JULIAN,
FOUND THIS USED BOOK,
IT WAS ONE OF MY
FAVORITIES! STEVE &
KAREN

A Long Vacation

by JULES VERNE

translated from the French
by Olga Marx

Holt, Rinehart and Winston
NEW YORK   CHICAGO   SAN FRANCISCO

Contents

Introduction

Jules Verne is famous throughout the world because he wrote about submarines and rockets as means of transportation long before such mechanisms had been invented, let alone constructed. But this man, who seldom left his own country, France, nor even had the wish to travel and explore foreign lands and the realms of sea and air which he described, also anticipated the more intangible aspects of modern life: the sociological and psychological approach which lies at the heart of the adventure tale *Deux Ans de Vacances*.

At the time of writing Jules Verne was about sixty. He had come to know his son's fifteen-year-old classmate Aristide Briand, who later became what the world still regards as the Secretary of Foreign Affairs *par excellence*. The sharp-tongued Clemenceau aptly said of him that he knew nothing and could accomplish everything. In this book Verne shows us Briand, whom he calls "Briant," as a typical French boy, not precisely industrious, but clever and resourceful, and gentle with the little boys who were among the passengers of the schooner *Sloughie*, bound on a vacation cruise and shipwrecked on an uninhabited island in the Pacific. He brings out Briant's character by contrasting him with an English and an American boy of about the same age. Thus he demonstrates the sociological principles which prevail in a colony of fourteen white boys and one Negro boy, all forced into close relationship by an unusual and threatening situation; and also their national characteristics and how they work out under these conditions. The psychology of the French, English, and American boy, stripped of adult hypocrisies and conventions, makes this adventure story intended for boys from ten to fourteen, of interest to their elders as well.

Sven-Erik Bergh, M.A. (Oxon.)

A Long Vacation

DESERT

Stop River

Wreck of
the *Severn*

North Creek

False
Sea
Point

TRAP WOODS

AUCKLAND HILL

TRAP WOODS

HOME

LAKE

Sloughie Bay

WOODS

Deception Bay

French Den

Wreck Coast

Zealand River

East River

THE DOWNS

SOUTH

MOORS

N

S

A Map of
Chairman Island

as reconstructed from the text

"I'll be all right, Jack." Briant put his arm round his brother. Then he pushed him gently aside and let himself drop overboard.

A moment later they saw him swimming vigorously, trailing the line behind him.

Even in calm weather his maneuver would have been risky. As it was, currents and crosscurrents kept him from going in a straight direction. Several times he was forced to skirt small whirlpools. Fifty feet of this, and he was exhausted. And suddenly he was being sucked into a boiling eddy of water.

"Help! Get me back!" he shouted with his last strength.

They hauled in the line with all their might.

"He's coming!"

"We've got him!"

"His eyes are shut. He's fainted!"

But when he was hoisted aboard Briant opened his eyes. He had only been unconscious for minutes. Jack rubbed him dry and brought him fresh clothing.

By this time it was noon and the tide was coming in. Since it was new moon it would rise even higher than usual. As bad luck would have it, the wind had freshened. A west wind. It lashed the sea and whipped up waves even taller, wilder, and stronger than those which had deposited the *Sloughie* between the reefs. She started rolling from side to side. The boys grabbed at whatever support they could find so as not to be washed overboard.

And then they screamed. A mountain was racing toward them, a mountain of water that must have been at least twenty feet high. It was topped with glaring white foam. On it came at a furious pace. It covered reefs and rocks. At the moment the boys thought their last, it lifted the *Sloughie* as if she weighed no more than a bird, and flung

her ashore only two hundred feet from the first trees at
the foot of the range. And there she lay, motionless, on
firm land this time, while the wave which had brought
her backed into the churning sea.

3

The Boys of Chairman School

The passengers on the *Sloughie* were all pupils of the
Chairman School, one of the best in Auckland, which was
at that time the capital of New Zealand. The school
numbered about a hundred pupils: English, French, American, and German. Its traditions and plans of study were
those current in the educational institutions of England.

It was located on Ika-Na-Mawi, one of the two main
islands of the New Zealand archipelago, separated from the
other, Tawaï-Ponamou, by Cook Strait. Their latitude,
between the thirty-fourth and forty-fifth parallel, was ap-
proximately that of France and North Africa.

Ika-Na-Mawi had a west and an east port. The latter, on
the Gulf of Hauraki, was shallow, but piers built out into
the water in the British manner made it possible for vessels
of medium tonnage to berth there. One of these piers,
Commercial Pier, was at the end of Queen's Street where
Chairman School was situated.

On February 15, 1860, crowds of boys and their parents
streamed out of the door. Vacation had begun, and they
were going home for two months of freedom and fun. A

small number of boys had a special pleasure in store. They were going on a six weeks' cruise.

The father of one of them, Mr. William Garnett, a retired captain in the merchant marines, owned a schooner, the *Sloughie,* and various families had joined to charter her to give their sons the opportunity to travel by sea in safety and comfort. Except for three of the boys, the passengers were English.

The boys who were to go on the cruise, came from various grades, or forms, as they are called in England. Their ages ranged from eight to fourteen.

Doniphan and his cousin Cross came of a family of rich landowners. They were both a little over thirteen and in the fifth form. Doniphan was easily the best student in the school. He was clever, industrious, and very careful about his person. A certain air of arrogance and the desire to dominate whatever group he was in had earned him the nickname of Lord Doniphan. Cross, a very average boy, admired and imitated him wherever he could.

Baxter, also thirteen, was in the same form. Level-headed and thoughtful, and a good worker, his chief gift was a flair for mechanics coupled with great skill in using his hands.

Webb and Wilcox, twelve and a half, were in the fourth form. They were both intelligent and willing, but apt to be quarrelsome, and known to be hard on their fags.

Garnett, the son of Captain Garnett, and Service were third formers and inseparable friends, always gay, always ingenious about shirking work and going off on affairs of their own. These generally involved some forbidden business. Garnett played the accordion and insisted on taking his instrument aboard the *Sloughie.* Service was the most

irresponsible boy in the school. He was really only there
in the flesh, for his mind was full of adventure stories
which occupied his waking hours and even slipped into
his dreams. His favorite books were *Robinson Crusoe* and
The Swiss Family Robinson.

Jenkins and Iverson, aged nine, were among the better
students of the school. Dole and Costar, eight and eight
and a half, were the youngest. Their outstanding characteristics were that Dole was pigheaded, and Costar
greedy and largely interested in food.

The three non-English boys on the *Sloughie* were
American and French. Gordon, fourteen, hailed from
Boston—a forthright "Yankee." He was an orphan, and
his elderly English guardian, a consul, had retired to New
Zealand and was having his ward educated at Chairman
School. Though not so brilliant as Doniphan, Gordon had
a good mind, plenty of common sense, resourcefulness,
and a strong feeling for justice and fairness. His informa-
tion in many fields, especially in botany and zoology,
was surprising, and he kept his facts as neatly arranged in
his brain as the papers and notebooks stowed in the cubby-
holes of his desk. Boys of all ages respected and liked him.

As for the two French boys, they were brothers, sons
of an engineer who had come to New Zealand to drain the
swamps in the interior of Ika-Na-Mawi Island.

Briant, the elder, thirteen, was very intelligent but so
unwilling to waste good time studying that he was usually
in the last quarter of his form. Occasionally he would
spurt into a period of concentrated work, and then his
quick understanding and remarkable memory helped him
outstrip the rest, even Doniphan, who resented such unexpected rivalry. He had none of the English boy's arrogance and was, in many ways, his opposite: careless in his

dress, a past master at all physical exploits, and a dare-
devil when it came to any enterprise which involved
danger. All this made for tension between the two, and
this tension was aggravated by Briant's opposition to
fagging, an attitude which made the little boys regard him
as their hero and protector.

Ten-year-old Jack, Briant's brother, was the most mis-
chievous boy in the school. There was no end to the
pranks he thought up, the tricks he played on his friends,
no end to his laughter and clowning. From the moment
the *Sloughie* was driven out to sea, however, his character
seemed to change so completely that not only Briant, but
everyone who knew him, was amazed and puzzled.

These then were the boys who had been fighting for
their lives against a storm far out at sea.

The route planned for the schooner was along the
coasts of New Zealand. She was a solidly-built vessel that
could hold her own even in the roughest weather. Besides
Captain Garnett, she was manned by six sailors, a cook,
and Moko, the cabin boy. Last but not least among the
passengers was Phann, a beautiful gundog from an American kennel. He belonged to Gordon and was never far
from his master.

The *Sloughie* was to leave on the sixteenth of February,
and the boys boarded the night before. The captain was
not due to arrive until sailing-time, and the crew were
having last drinks at one of the many bars near the port.
Only the helmsman and Moko were aboard to receive the
passengers and, after these had gone to bed, the helmsman
decided to spend the evening in town at a cabaret. He
intended to return after an hour or so, but lost track of
the time. As for Moko, when there was no more for him
to do, he, too, went to bed.

What happened then no one knew. Only one thing was certain: either through negligence in the way her lines had been secured, or by some deliberate and malicious act the *Sloughie* broke loose from her piling. It was a starless night. The port and the Gulf of Hauraki lay in darkness. The wind freshened, and the schooner, caught in a strong current, was swept out to sea.

When Moko woke she was rolling and pitching. He knew at once that she would not behave like that in port, ran up on deck, and saw she was loose.

At his cries Briant, Gordon, and Doniphan jumped out of bed and joined him on deck. They called for help. Their voices were drowned by the crash of waves and the roaring wind. Not a single light from the city was visible. The schooner was already three miles out from the coast.

At Briant's suggestion the boys, together with Moko, tried to hoist a sail in order to get back to port. But they were too inexperienced and accomplished the opposite of what they had set out to do. The *Sloughie* was carried farther and farther out to sea. She rounded Cape Colville and was soon many miles away from New Zealand.

Briant and his companions realized that no aid could come to them from land. A passing vessel was their only hope. But would such a vessel see a small schooner in the dark? However slim the chance of meeting with a steamer, Moko nevertheless fastened a lantern to the mizzenmast. Then they waited.

Luckily, the little boys had not wakened. They would only have been in the way, and their fright would have made matters more difficult. They were allowed to sleep on.

Faster and faster went the *Sloughie*. Helplessly the boys waited for the dawn.

"A light!" Moko suddenly shouted. "A white light! That means it's a steamer."

Soon they saw two more lights, a red and a green. These indicated the direction. Since both were visible at the same time, they knew that the steamer was heading straight for the *Sloughie*. The distance between the two vessels grew rapidly less. The boys started calling again. Evidently no one heard. But there was the lantern! Surely some sailor would see the lantern! And then this last hope was destroyed. A wild lurch shook the schooner from end to end. The lantern rocked madly—and fell into the sea. In complete darkness, with nothing to show her presence, the *Sloughie* raced along at twelve knots. In a few minutes the steamer was up with her, grazed her stern, and was gone. The shock had been so slight, it had not even been noticed by the crew of the eight- or nine-hundred-ton steamer. That it had sliced off part of the name of the *Sloughie* also went unnoticed, even by the boys. They had been so sure they would be saved. Now they were in despair, particularly when Moko, a much-traveled boy, told them that not many steamers plying between America and Australia were likely to pass. They took more northerly or more southerly routes.

It was then that Briant, with an energy beyond his years, took charge. Even Doniphan could not escape the influence of his cool and calm acceptance of the situation. Though he did not know enough to be able to head the schooner west, he watched day and night, and remembered to toss bottles, which contained messages on the *Sloughie's* plight, into the ocean.

In the meantime, a westerly wind drove the schooner faster and faster. Monstrous waves threatened to swallow

her up at any moment. The rest has been told: the *Sloughie*
was cast ashore on an unknown beach in the Pacific.

In Auckland the disappearance of the schooner was
discovered the night of the fourteenth. Whether her lines
had broken, whether someone had tampered with them,
nobody knew. Two small steamers were immediately sent
in search of the schooner. They went miles beyond the
gulf and saw nothing of her. All they found was bits of
floating wreckage. Part of a plank bore three or four
letters which pointed to the name *Sloughie*. They reported
their find, and everyone concluded that the schooner had
been smashed to bits by the stormy sea. The families of
the boys gave them up for lost, and the entire city of
Auckland went into mourning.

4

Ground Underfoot

The coast was deserted. It was an hour since the schooner
had been thrust aground and yet no one had appeared to
investigate. There was no sign of a house, a cabin, or a
hut, nor a footprint on the beach streaked with long
chains of seaweed. No fishing boat rocked at the mouth
of the river, and they could not detect a single thread of
smoke between the south and north promontories of the
bay.

"Well, at least we're on land. That's something,"
Gordon said. "Even if it does seem to be uninhabited."

"The main thing is for it to be habitable," Briant

declared. "We have provisions and ammunition for quite a while. What we need right now is some sort of shelter, especially for the Elbees."

"As for finding out just where we are, that can wait till we have a place where we can sleep and eat. If we're on a continent, we have a good chance of being rescued. If it's an island . . . an uninhabited island . . ." Briant broke off. "Come on, Gordon," he cried. "I can't wait, after all. Let's make sure right now. This minute!"

In a quarter of an hour they had reached the woods between the range of rocks and the right bank of the river. They made their way round fallen branches crumbling with age, and waded knee-deep through the withered leaves of countless years. There was no path, not even the hint of a trail. Birds took startled flight at their approach, but this did not necessarily mean that they had been hunted by people who lived there. Natives from a nearby territory might have visited from time to time.

The woods grew denser as they neared the cliffs which rose to a height of about eighty feet.

"If only we could find a cave here," Gordon exclaimed. "What with those trees growing thick to keep off the sea wind, it would make a perfect shelter until we explore beyond the range and see what the interior's like."

"How are you going to get beyond?"

It was an apt question. The range was a solid stone wall. Not only was there no cave, there were not even footholds for climbing to the top to reconnoiter. They decided to skirt the base and noticed that, while the right bank of the river was green and shaded by trees, the left was a vast swamp stretching south to the horizon.

When they returned from their unsuccessful search, they found Jenkins, Iverson, Dole, and Costar busy collecting clams and mussels. Gordon motioned to the older boys.

"No luck," he told them. "We'll have to live on the *Sloughie* until we find something better."

"She's listing badly to larboard."

"I know, but she's buried so deep that nothing will move her, at least not for a long time."

"She'll never sail again," Service said sadly.

"We can use her as she is, though," Gordon insisted. "Some of the cabins are all right, and the kitchen's in fine shape."

This cheered the Elbees, who had left their shell hunting to listen. They at once began to talk about food, and each described what he particularly liked to eat, until they were all so hungry that they decided to have a meal then and there.

A rope-ladder enabled everyone to scramble aboard and Moko, who as a cabin boy had often helped in the kitchen, set to work with pots and pans. Service, who admitted that cooking was a hobby of his, took a hand, and soon they were all happily eating. All except Jack who continued moody and silent. When asked what was the matter, he said, "Nothing," and no one could get another word out of him.

When darkness fell, they were so tired they could think only of sleep. Briant, Gordon, and Doniphan took turns on watch, but all remained quiet; neither wild beasts nor fierce natives appeared.

The next morning they decided to take stock of whatever provisions and equipment the *Sloughie* held. Doniphan, who was an excellent shot, had, to be sure, seen a number of birds, but just game-birds and edible shells would be monotonous in the long run. Besides, the boys knew that meat and seafood alone were not enough to give them a good, all-around diet.

"There must be a lot of tinned vegetables and things," someone suggested.

"If the tins haven't been knocked flat," Baxter replied.

"If they've been damaged, couldn't we boil up what's left and use it just the same?" Service asked.

"I'll see to that," Moko promised.

"We ought to get at it at once then," Briant said. "Because for the first few days at any rate we'll have to live off the *Sloughie*."

"How about eggs?" Wilcox asked. "There ought to be eggs on the rocks to the north of the bay. That's where the sea birds lay."

"Hurrah for eggs!" Dole and Costar cried enthusiastically.

"And we could fish," Webb suggested. "We have tackle aboard, and there are plenty of fish in the sea. Who wants to go fishing?"

"Me! Me!" the younger boys shouted.

"All right," Briant said. "But look, it's not a game. Only those who want to fish in good earnest may have rods and reels."

"We'll treat fishing as if it were a job," Iverson promised.

"There's not only food to think of," Gordon reminded them. "We need a lot of other things to live. You go and get fish and clams or whatever you want for lunch, while we find out what there is on the *Sloughie*."

"Moko, you go with them," Briant said in a low voice. "Take care of the Elbees."

"You can trust me," Moko whispered back. He was especially devoted to Briant, who liked and treated him as a friend.

"Come on," Jenkins cried.

"Aren't you going with them, Jack?" Briant asked.

"No." Jack spoke without any expression. A moment later he went off by himself.

As soon as the Elbees were out of sight, the older boys started on their survey. Silently they passed by the spare sails, the lines, and everything needed for navigation, for they well knew that they could not repair the *Sloughie* and make her seaworthy again.

"I'll make a note of them just the same," Gordon said. "Who knows what we might need the canvas for!"

Practical and methodical, like most American boys, he got out his notebook and began making lists.

Under the heading "arms" he put down eight rifles, one long-range duck-gun, a dozen pistols, and the two small cannons of the *Sloughie*. Under "ammunition," a large quantity of buckshot and bullets, two kegs of powder, weighing about twenty-five pounds each, and about thirty cannon cartridges and projectiles.

There was a large assortment of tools, household utensils, linen, blankets, and clothing, including wool jerseys, oilskins and hoods, as well as cotton shirts. Though part of the vessel had been crushed by the shock which hurled her ashore, most of the schooner and her contents were in good condition. There were enough supplies to last a long time, a very long time. The unspoken word in everyone's mind was: "Forever?"

Gordon did not give them time to brood.

"Two aneroid barometers," he announced, as he scribbled in his book.

"Whatever that may mean!" Wilcox remarked.

"It's a barometer with a needle connected to the top of a metal box that has no air in it," Garnett explained. "I know, because my dad told me. A change in pressure makes the needle move, because then the elastic top of the box bends in and out."

"Two clocks, two copper foghorns, three binoculars," Gordon went on. "A compass, and several inflatable canoes to cross rivers or lakes."

In the ship's library they found maps and two atlases. One of them was that by Stieler, the best in modern geography. There were a number of works of fiction in both French and English, among them *Robinson Crusoe* and *The Swiss Family Robinson*, books on science and travel, and a calendar of 1860.

"I'll cross out the days," Baxter volunteered. "So we don't lose track of the time." And he immediately drew a thick line through the tenth of March, the day the *Sloughie* was wrecked.

Gordon quietly went on with his list: writing materials and paper, hardware, sewing-kit, signal flags of the kind boats use to communicate with each other at sea, flares to be used by night, many tins of food and boxes of biscuits, and a supply of brandy to be used in emergencies.

When his first rough draft was complete he announced that the fifteen survivors of the *Sloughie* need have no fears for months to come. In all honesty he added that, even with all the tools and material at hand, none of them had the know-how to repair the *Sloughie*, or to build a vessel large and sturdy enough to sail the Pacific; that the lifeboats had been torn from the deck by the storm and swept out to sea, and what remained in the way of craft was a yawl, fit only to navigate along the coast.

This put everyone in a sober mood, and they were glad when, toward noon, the Elbees, guided by Moko, rushed up loaded with clams, mussels, and even oysters.

"And there must be simply millions of eggs!" Costar shouted. "We saw flocks and flocks of pigeons!"

"Their nests are up on the rocks," Moko said. "We could climb with the help of a rope."

"Why not shoot the pigeons!" Doniphan cried. "Webb, Cross, Wilcox, will you join me?" The three were more than ready.

"Don't shoot too many," Briant warned. "We have to go easy on the ammunition. Anyway, we know where to find them, if we need more."

"I really don't need any advice," Doniphan said. "This isn't my first hunting trip. We'll go right after lunch."

Although the position of the schooner made the dining room table stand at a slant, they all enjoyed what the younger boys had collected, plus tinned corned-beef and a great many biscuits.

The afternoon was spent arranging their supplies, while Doniphan and his friends hunted, and the Elbees fished. They were too busy to think of their plight, but every once in a while Gordon would pause in his work and look thoughtful, Baxter would frown, and Service sigh.

If only we were grown up, Briant thought. We might have a chance. But the oldest of us is barely fourteen. What if we should have to spend years and years here! Why, you're afraid! he told himself. Then he straightened proudly. Only a fool would not be afraid, he decided. And only a coward would give way to fear and despair.

Quietly he put his whole strength to stacking the heavy boxes of cartridges.

5

The Lie of the Land

Whatever they had landed on, island or continent, the survivors of the *Sloughie* were certainly not in the tropics. Oaks, beeches, alders, and birches do not grow in regions of the central Pacific. The vegetation pointed to a higher latitude than that of New Zealand. They were nearer the South Pole and that meant that the winter would be long and severe.

Briant, Gordon, and Doniphan, whose intelligence and strength of character stamped them as leaders, thought seriously of what the future held in store.

The trees were already shedding their leaves. Gordon cradled a golden birch leaf in his hand.

"Island or no island, I don't think we ought to settle on this part of the coast," he said.

"Just what I was thinking," Doniphan agreed. "If we stay here till the weather gets rough it'll be too late to travel what may turn out to be hundreds of miles to reach some inhabited place."

"It's only the middle of March," Briant reminded them.

"The mild season may well last until the end of April," Doniphan said. "That gives us six whole weeks. We can go a long way in that time."

"If there is a way!" Briant objected.

"Why shouldn't there be!"

"Even if there is a way," Gordon put in, "how do we know where it would take us?"

"All I say," Doniphan insisted, "is that it would be crazy

not to leave the schooner before cold and rain set in, and that there's no sense in seeing nothing but difficulties at every step."

"Better see them than start off like fools in a country of which we know nothing," Briant said.

"It's easy to call people fools when they don't agree with you," Doniphan remarked pointedly.

"Quarreling isn't going to improve matters," Gordon interrupted quickly. "Let's get together on this. Doniphan's right in saying that, if we are near an inhabited region, there's no time to lose getting to it. Briant, though, is justified in asking whether or not it's possible."

"If we bear north and then south to head east, we should soon come to . . ." Doniphan began.

"That would work on a continent," Briant cut in. "Not on an island."

"We've got to find out what it is," Gordon said. "We can't leave the *Sloughie* till we know if there's sea in the east."

"It's the *Sloughie* that will leave us," Doniphan protested. "She can't hold out against the kind of winter storms which are sure to come here."

"Agreed," Gordon said. "Still, if we're going to explore the interior, we first have to know where we're going."

Doniphan nodded reluctantly.

"I'm willing to make a reconnaissance trip," Briant offered.

"So am I," Doniphan said quickly.

"I'm sure we'd all be willing," Gordon said. "But since we can't possibly take the Elbees on a long tiring trip, only two or three of us will be able to go."

"It's too bad there's not a good lookout," Briant said. "A high hill from where we could see around."

"Why don't we go north?" Gordon asked. "The northern promontory ends in a cliff. I should say it's two hundred and fifty to three hundred feet high. From up there we could see what's on the other side of the rock-range."

"See what?" Doniphan said.

"Whatever there is," Briant said rather shortly.

"It's not such a long way off," Gordon said. "One could easily go there and back in a day. Seven or eight miles, perhaps, five as the crow flies."

Although Doniphan objected on principle, because it hadn't been his idea, they decided to make the attempt.

But the next morning and for five days, the weather crossed their plans. It rained a thin, steady rain. It was foggy. Even had they reached the top of the cliff, they could not have seen a thing.

To make at least some use of the delay, they busied themselves trying on the warm clothing they found in various lockers. The older boys fitted themselves out fairly well. With the Elbees it was another story.

Briant, who had a gift and a need for taking care of those younger than he, felt deeply responsible for them. Yet here was a task which he could not tackle. All he could do was to cut down pants and sleeves. It was Moko who came to the rescue. As a cabin boy he could do a little of everything, so now he turned tailor and used his needle and thread to such good purpose that soon Costar, Dole, Jenkins, and Iverson were equipped for cold weather. There was a great deal of laughing as they tried on their new outfits. Only Jack did not join in. It was not only that, at ten, he did not quite belong to the Elbee group, nor yet to that of the older boys. He was brooding over something else, and several times Briant noticed that his eyes were red, as if he'd been crying.

"Does anything hurt?" he asked. "Don't you feel well?"

"I'm perfectly all right," Jack answered, and slipped away as soon as his brother's back was turned.

As for Doniphan, Wilcox, Webb, and Cross, they spent those days from the eleventh to the fifteenth of March hunting. Doniphan was a splendid shot, with Cross, his cousin, who applauded everything he did, a close second. Webb was fair, but Wilcox, less experienced than the others, suggested traps and snares, a notion indignantly spurned by the rest.

Gordon felt uneasy as they went off together. At a time when it was of the greatest importance to be united, those four were forming a solid group which tended to keep apart. When he had once mentioned this hesitatingly to Doniphan, his words had been met with cold silence.

The hunters returned with a good bag which would help stretch the supplies of the *Sloughie*. There were pigeons, ducks, and geese, as well as a few gulls, cormorants, and oyster catchers which Moko declared inedible.

"That's just because you don't know how to prepare them," Cross said loftily.

All this time Briant saw to it that the Elbees were kept so busy they wouldn't feel homesick. Either Garnett or Baxter took them fishing or clam digging.

"It's like a picnic that's going on and on," Costar said happily. It never occurred to him that it might not end at all!

The fifteenth of March promised fair weather. The fog had lifted during the night. A wind scattered the last shreds of mist. By noon the sun broke through. The barometer was rising steadily. Briant was determined to leave the next day, and to leave alone. Only Gordon knew that he intended to go at dawn. The two would have liked to go together, but then there would have been no one left behind to take responsibility for the group. It had been Briant's idea to find out whether there was sea in the east. He set out so early that no one saw him go.

He took with him a stout stick, a pistol, the best of the three binoculars on the *Sloughie,* and a bag with biscuits, salt meat, and a gourd of water.

To make the most of the clear weather he walked quickly. If the east grew foggy by afternoon, the whole undertaking would be scotched.

Going along the coast was so easy, he thought he might reach the promontory before eight. But when he came to where the rock-range stood close to the reefs, he was faced with difficulties. The strip of more or less firm sand narrowed. He was constantly held up by swirls of slimy seaweed, slippery rocks, stones that gave under his feet, and deep pools he was obliged to skirt.

All these obstacles delayed him a good two hours. This part of the coast must have been under water at high tide. He would have to return before the beach was again submerged. Shoes and socks in his hand, Briant slithered over the wet rocks.

Although he had to look where he was going to avoid falls, he observed as much he could of his surroundings. Birds were particularly plentiful over this part of the bay. Flock after flock of ducks circled over his head. He also saw five or six seals sunning on a sandbank. Since they did not seem at all disturbed by his approach, he concluded that they had never had cause to fear man. The seals were interesting for another reason, too: they told him something about the place. Their presence meant that the *Sloughie* must have been wrecked nearer to the South Pole than the boys had supposed. A crowd of penguins, birds which inhabit Antarctic regions, confirmed Briant's guess. They waddled past by the hundreds, flapping their short wings, rather more like flippers, and used for swimming, not flying.

It was ten o'clock, and Briant, hungry and tired, decided to make a stop and eat before attempting the climb up the cliff. Alone, miles away from his companions, he sat down and coolly sized up the situation: the dangers they might encounter, the hardships sure to be in store, Doniphan's hostile attitude, and the peculiar behavior of his brother Jack. The boy had some secret on his mind. Briant was determined to force it out of him.

After an hour's rest, he slung his bag over his shoulder and began the ascent. He noticed that the cliff was not of limestone like those along the Channel in Western Europe, but of granite. The rocks were often so far apart that Briant, though he was a good climber, could barely grip the edge of the one above to hoist himself up. A fall would have meant instant death. At last he reached the summit and immediately trained his binoculars on the east.

The range was the only elevated portion on a plateau which sloped gently to the interior. Vast forests, yellowed by autumn, hid the rivers that flowed to the sea. He saw miles and miles of land stretching toward the horizon. To know what lay east would require a longer trip. Toward the north there was what looked like a sandy desert, toward the south a limitless swamp.

Briant still could not tell whether he was on an island or a continent. If it was an island, it was a very large one. Looking to the west again he suddenly saw three black dots on the sea. They shone brightly in the slant rays of the sun which had already passed its zenith.

"Ships!" he exclaimed aloud. "Passing ships!" They were

at least fifteen miles off. Then he grew doubtful. Perhaps the brilliant light had produced an optical illusion.

He wiped the glasses clouded by his breath, and looked again.

Those three dots must be ships. Only the hulls were visible, and there was no smoke to indicate they were steamers. In any case, they were much too far away for anyone to see him wave, or to hear him call. It was important for him to get back as fast as possible, so they could light a big signal fire on the shore.

He kept staring at those three black dots, and suddenly he realized they were not moving. They remained fixed, as if nailed to the spot. They were not ships after all. Just three small islands west of where the *Sloughie* lay.

Briant was bitterly disappointed, but he had no time to give himself up to his dark mood. It was two o'clock and low tide. Now was the moment for him to start back. One more look, he decided, and then he would climb down. The light had changed. He might see something that had escaped him before.

He did, but what he saw only made his mood blacker. Beyond the last rim of green in the east was a clear blue line. It seemed to curve and disappear in a confusion of trees and creepers. His hand began to shake. He all but dropped the binoculars. What he saw was the sea! The *Sloughie* was not on a continent. She was on an island in an enormous ocean, an island which her survivors had not the means to leave. His breath came in gasps. Then he got hold of himself. He would not let himself be crushed by the thought of the future.

Fifteen minutes later he had reached the foot of the cliff. Before five he had arrived at the *Sloughie* where all were awaiting him impatiently.

6

A Big Catch

Briant looked at their eager and anxious faces. It was not easy for him to say: "We're on an island!"

Briefly he told them the results of his reconnoitering: that in the east, beyond the forest zone, he had seen water curving from north to south—the sea, and that now their only hope of rescue was a passing ship.

"You could have been mistaken," Doniphan objected heatedly. "Maybe you just thought you saw it."

"No, I'm positive. What I saw was water."

"Perhaps you took a cloud bank for the sea," Cross said. Briant did not answer.

"How far off was it?" Wilcox asked.

"About six miles from the cape."

"And there weren't any mountains in between? Or hills?" Webb wanted to know.

"Nothing but the sky."

Briant was so certain that further doubt seemed unreasonable, yet Doniphan persisted.

"I won't believe what you say until I've looked with my own eyes," he said obstinately.

"We'll go and see for ourselves and then you'll be satisfied," Gordon promised.

"What I say is that there's not a day to lose," Baxter put in. "Just in case we're on a continent and want to get away from here before winter . . ."

"We'll go tomorrow," Gordon said. "And plan on several days. There's an 'if,' of course. The weather! We'll

go if the weather's fair. To try and cross the forest in a
storm would be taking too much of a risk."

"Agreed," Briant said. "Maybe we shall see land beyond
our island."

"Assuming it *is* an island," Doniphan said and shrugged.

"I tell you it is!" Briant was losing his patience.

"Don't tell me you're so perfect you can't make mistakes!"

"I certainly can and do make mistakes. But this time I'm
right. I'll go back to that water I saw, and if Doniphan
wants to come with me . . ."

"I do."

"So do we!" shouted the other boys.

"Let's be sensible about it," Gordon said. "We can't all
go. The Elbees couldn't make it, and we can't leave them
alone on the *Sloughie*. How about Doniphan, Briant and
two others going?"

"Me!" Wilcox shouted.

"I want to go, too," Service said.

"Four of you then," Gordon said. "So there'll be enough
of us here to send a search party out for you if you stay
away too long. A few of us have to be with the schooner.
She's our home, after all!"

Once more Gordon had succeeded in averting an open
quarrel between Briant and Doniphan. Now, to take their
minds off their resentment, he began to speak of what they
might find when they reached their goal. An island, perhaps, separated from theirs by a narrow channel of water
which would be easy to cross. Their own island might be
part of an archipelago. One thing was certain, and no one
contradicted: there was no land in the west between New
Zealand and whatever coast they were on. Their only hope
lay in the east.

Stieler's atlas, which they had found in the library, contained a number of maps of the Pacific. They pored over
them. On the route from Auckland to South America they
found the Tuamotou Archipelago, and east of it Easter
Island and also the island of Juan Fernandez where Selkirk,
a true Crusoe, had passed a good part of his life. South
there was only the Antarctic Ocean, to the east the Chiloë
group scattered along the coast of Chile, and lower the
islands of the Strait of Magellan, south of which lay
the Tierra del Fuego Archipelago buffeted by the stormy
seas of Cape Horn. If the schooner had been wrecked on
one of those uninhabited islands, they were hundreds of
miles from Chile, La Plata, or Argentina, miles of immense
solitude and unknown dangers.

All this made the four boys more anxious than ever to
start on the trip, but again the weather held them up. They
woke to fog and rain, and gusts of cold wind. While they
chafed at the delay, in their hearts they were not entirely
sorry to put off confirming Briant's statement that they
were on an island.

While they waited for the weather to clear, they found
plenty to do. The *Sloughie*, already badly damaged by the
shock of being cast ashore, was in no condition to take the
torrents of rain and the violent squalls. Seams needed to be
caulked, planking repaired. The decks were in bad shape
and—forced to it by sheer necessity—they covered them
with the spare sails on which they counted for making
tents. The need for a waterproof shelter became more glaring day by day.

Whenever the rain let up a little, Doniphan, Webb, and
Wilcox went hunting. Gordon, who wished to split up
Doniphan's tight group, especially asked Cross to help Gar-

nett and Service take care of the Elbees who wanted to
fish. Jack joined them only when his brother insisted.

Shoals of small fish, which could be scooped up in the
hand, swarmed between the masses of kelp that clung to
the reefs. The larger fish were caught with a line or with
nets.

"I've caught one!" Jenkins shouted. "A regular whop-
per!"

"Mine's bigger," Iverson claimed.

"Hey, mine's getting away!" Costar shrieked, and Garnett came to the rescue.

"Pull!" he said. "Pull hard!"

It was important to drag the full nets in at once, for fierce
lampreys lurked in the clear water and often devoured the
fish before they could be brought ashore.

The best fish caught were silver hake which tasted excellent fresh and could be salted down for future use.

One afternoon—it was the twenty-seventh of March—
they made another much bigger catch.

Gordon, Briant, Service, and Moko were working on the
Sloughie when they heard excited shouts.

"Quick! Come quick!" Jenkins cried.

"Come and see Costar taking a ride," Iverson called.

"Hurry, Briant, or it'll get away," Jenkins urged.

"I've had enough of it." This was Costar's voice. "Get me
down. I'm scared!"

"Giddup!" Dole had climbed up behind Costar on some
huge, moving object.

It was a tortoise! But what a tortoise! Usually one sees
them floating on the sea asleep. This one had been surprised
on the beach and was trying to get back where it belonged.
The Elbees had put a rope round its neck, but the tortoise

was so enormous and of such giant strength that, instead of being pulled back by the boys, it was pulling them.

"It's going to drown us!" Costar shrieked in terror.

"All you have to do is get off!" Briant reassured him, and only then did the two boys let themselves drop to the sand. The tortoise kept on going.

"We must catch it," said Gordon. "It's good food, and lots of it."

"No use trying to shoot it," Service said. "That shell's bulletproof."

"And if we go at it with a hatchet, it'll just draw in its head," Garnett said.

"There's only one way," Gordon stated. "I've read about it. We have to turn it over."

"Spars are what we need for that," Briant said, and Moko ran to the schooner to fetch them.

When he returned, the tortoise was only about thirty feet from the water and all the boys hanging on together could not hold it back. On the contrary: the tortoise was pulling them along. The animal could probably have dragged twice as many boys into the sea.

They managed to put two spars under its belly. With these as levers, they were finally able to turn the tortoise on its back. It could not right itself, and before it could retract its head, Briant dealt it a sharp blow. It died on the instant.

"Well, Costar," he asked, "are you still afraid?"

"Not a bit, Briant. Now that it's dead . . ."

"I'll bet you don't dare eat it," Service teased.

"Can you eat it?"

"You certainly can."

"If it tastes good I'll eat it," Costar declared.

Since it was impossible to either carry or haul the tortoise to the schooner, it had to be carved up on the spot. The boys did not like the idea, but they had found out that disagreeable tasks just had to be dealt with when it was a question of getting food to live on.

The most difficult problem was how to get off the shell. It was as hard as iron. Finally they pried it off by inserting a chisel in the cracks between the separate slabs of shell. By the time they had finished, they had fifty pounds of meat, a valuable addition to their larder. They discovered that both turtle soup and steak was delicious, even though Service had charred the meat more than a little when he broiled it over hot coals. Everyone, including Phann, who came in for many scraps, ate with relish.

A few days after this novel and excellent dinner, the barometer rose at last. It was the first of April.

"I believe we could start tomorrow," Doniphan said.

"Didn't you say that the water you saw was about six or seven miles from the promontory?" Gordon asked Briant.

"Yes, but since the bay has deep bends, it may be less if we went straight from here."

"Do you think you'll be gone over twenty-four hours?"

"Not if we can go directly east. Once we've skirted the rocks, though, we'll have to find a way through the forests."

"That shouldn't be hard," Doniphan said.

"Maybe not. But suppose we have to face up to a river, or swamps! I think we ought to take food for several days with us."

"And ammunition," Wilcox added.

"Of course," Briant said. "And look, Gordon, if we aren't back by forty-eight hours, don't start worrying."

"I'd worry even if you weren't gone for more than half a day," Gordon answered. "But that's neither here nor there. This expedition has to be made. And not only to find out whether what you saw is the sea. It's almost as important to know what the country's like beyond the range. We didn't find a cave on this side, and we can't camp out in the cold when we leave the *Sloughie*."

"You're right," Briant said. "We'll keep our eyes open for some place."

"That is, in case we are not able to leave this so-called 'island,' " Doniphan could not resist saying.

"Quite so," Gordon said dryly. "And don't forget, that winter will be here before we can undertake the long trek you have in mind—even if we are on a continent."

He was sorry he was not to be of the party, not only because he would miss the adventure, but because he would not be there to keep the peace between Briant and Doniphan. During the evening he managed to have a few words alone with Briant and made him promise to avoid any word or act which might lead to a quarrel.

The night was clear and still. The stars and constellations of that part of the world blazed in ancient glory. Among them was the Southern Cross which shines over the Antarctic.

As the boys looked up at it they thought of home and of their country which they might, perhaps, never see again.

"Let's go to bed," Briant urged. "We want to make an early start."

7

What Lay in the East

Briant, Doniphan, Wilcox, and Service set out at seven. The sky was cloudless. It was neither too hot nor too cold. If anything came up to delay them, it would certainly not be the weather.

Gordon made Phann go with them. The dog's keen sense of hearing and smell would make him a useful member of the expedition.

They made straight for the range which they intended skirting toward the cape in the north of the bay, unless they found some way of scaling the rocks before they got there.

It was not long before they reached the place where Briant and Gordon had stopped on their first exploring trip, and they wasted a good half hour looking for some pass across, or for projections which would make it possible for them to climb. After a vain search they had to resign themselves to the long detour.

"We'll have to hurry because of the tide," Briant warned. "If we don't make it through at low tide, we'll lose half a day."

"Suppose the tide does come in while we're on the march," Wilcox said cockily. "The worst that can happen is that we'll get our ankles wet."

"Ankles and chest, and then you'll be in water up to the ears," Briant answered. "The tide rises at least five or six feet. We'd have done better to try for the cape without putting time on trying to find somewhere to cross."

"It was up to you," Doniphan said. "You're the guide

on this trip, and if we're delayed by the tide it'll be your fault."

"All right, Doniphan. So it will. In any case, don't let's lose another minute."

"Where's Service?" Wilcox suddenly exclaimed.

"Just a few minutes ago I saw him and Phann going off to the right," Doniphan remembered.

"Service! Service!" they called.

At first there was no reply. Then they heard cries and barks, and ran to the rescue—or so they thought—only to find Service safe and sound, and almost dancing with excitement.

"Look!" he cried. "Look what I've found!"

He pointed to a wide, irregular cleft in the wall. The pounding rains of perhaps hundreds of years had eroded the rock and opened a funnel-shaped path to the top of the range. The sides were rough and provided a series of footholds for climbing. The only danger was that the boys' weight and movements might cause a stone-slide. They decided to take that risk.

Doniphan was the first to swing upward from a pile of rubble.

"Careful, be careful!" Briant called to him, but Doniphan forged ahead. He had set his heart on being braver than the rest, above all braver than Briant. Soon he was halfway up. The others followed, keeping well behind him, so as not to be hit by falling stones. By the time they reached the top Doniphan had already taken the binoculars from their case and trained them on the east.

"Well?" Wilcox asked impatiently. "What do you see?"

"Forests and sky," Doniphan answered. "Nothing else." He handed the glasses to Wilcox.

"Not a sign of water!" Wilcox declared.

"See for yourself, Briant," Doniphan said in a self-satisfied voice, "and you'll have to admit that you were mistaken."

"I wasn't," Briant insisted. "I was on the cape. The cape's higher than here. I could see farther."

"We'll not just take your word for it, anyway."

"You don't have to. Now that we've crossed the range we can cut through the forest and go straight on to the sea."

"All right," Doniphan said. "It can't be too far. Though, if you ask me, it's hardly worth the trouble."

"Stay here, then," Briant said calmly, mindful of his promise to Gordon. "Service and I can go on alone. We want to see what the country's like—quite apart from getting to the sea."

"No, let's all go together," Wilcox said hastily. "But first let's have lunch."

Half an hour later they were on their way.

The first mile or so was through short grass. Here and there were hummocks covered with moss and lichen, and clumps of holly and barberry bushes. When they hit the dry bed of a stream, the going grew easier still.

Only when they reached the forest, did they run up against obstacles. Fallen trees blocked the way. They often had to use their hatchets to hack through thickets of briars. Soon their arms were more weary than their legs, and the advance was so slow that they made hardly more than three miles from lunch till evening.

In all this time they had seen no trace of any human being. The trees had been felled by storms, the trodden patches in the grass pointed to some not very large animals. Once in a while they caught a glimpse of creatures running, but they were too far away to make out what

they were. The birds they saw tested Doniphan's self-
control to the utmost. There were partridges and quail,
wild geese and grouse. But he curbed his desire to shoot,
for a shot would have alerted natives—if there were any
about.

"If we camped here there'd always be plenty of food,"
he stated.

After trekking through beeches and cypresses perhaps
a hundred feet high, and sniffing at some magnificent trees
whose bark smelled like cinnamon, they called a second
halt in a clearing by a shallow creek. The clear water
flowed gently over a bed of black pebbles. It would have
been easy to cross almost anywhere, but at one point a
number of large, flat stones afforded dry passage.

"That's odd," Doniphan remarked. "They're placed so
evenly."

"Almost a bridge," Wilcox said.

"They couldn't have put themselves there like that,"
Briant speculated.

They examined the arrangement of the stones closely,
but could not decide whether hands or flood waters had
made the bridge, especially as neither the right nor the
left bank yielded any sign of man.

The creek flowed northeast. Did it empty into the sea
Briant claimed to have seen from the cape? None of the
boys wanted to reopen that particular argument.

"It could be the tributary of a river," Doniphan suggested. "Since it flows in an easterly direction, why don't
we just follow it?"

Toward half past five both he and Briant noted that
the creek made a sharp turn to the north. To go east they
had to abandon it, so they struck out and were soon walking in tall grasses which sometimes closed over their heads.

They had to keep calling to one another to make sure they were still keeping together.

As Briant walked on he began to feel misgivings. After almost a whole day's march, there was still nothing that gave any inkling the sea might be near. What if he had been mistaken after all? He shut his eyes for a moment and again saw the blue line, the line that curved! It *was* water, he told himself decisively.

When seven o'clock came and they were still not out of the forest, they resolved to spend the night there. They had plenty of corned-beef and biscuits for supper, and good blankets to keep them warm.

"We could light a fire, too," Service said. "To frighten animals off."

"And give us away to the natives," Doniphan objected, and Briant agreed with him.

They had just decided to sleep under a big beech when Wilcox found what, in the dusk, looked like a tall thicket round a tree with lowhanging branches. They crept in and found a thick carpet of dry leaves. Tired out by the day they soon fell asleep and even Phann, who was supposed to watch over his masters, followed suit.

It was seven before they woke. The sun was slanting through the leaves. Service was the first to get up.

"Briant! Doniphan!" he cried out in amazement. "Look where we've been sleeping!"

All drowsiness was gone at once. The boys opened their eyes and blinked: they were in a hut! A hut made of interlaced branches, the kind of shelter the South American Indians call *ajoupa*. It seemed to have been made long ago, and had withstood wind and rain thanks to the fact that it was built against a trunk which had both sheltered and supported it.

"Then there *are* people here," Doniphan said, casting a quick glance around.

"At least there were, at some time or other," Briant said thoughtfully.

"That would explain the bridge over the creek," Wilcox added.

"It's all to the good," Service announced happily. "If there are natives they are good people who put up this shelter so we could pass a peaceful night in it."

"They weren't thinking of us," Doniphan said. "And I don't know about their goodness. For all we know, they may be headhunters or cannibals."

There was a moment's silence while the boys considered this possibility.

"Let's see if we can find something in the hut that would give us an idea who they were," Briant proposed.

They turned over every inch of the litter of leaves, and in one corner Service did actually find a shard of baked clay that seemed to be part of a bowl. Besides being added proof that men had lived there, however, it told them nothing at all.

Half an hour later, compass in hand, they set out towards the east. The journey continued slow and difficult. It was ten o'clock by the time they reached the edge of the forest. Instead of a vault of green boughs they saw blue sky over a stretch of flat land covered with wild thyme and ferns. And then they heard a sound. It recurred at short intervals. They stood and listened. There was no room for doubt. What they heard was surf beating on a shore. A few steps more, and they saw a strip of sand.

Doniphan was silent. It was hard for him to admit that Briant had been right.

As for Briant, he did not want an outspoken admission.

There was no hint of triumph in either his face or bearing. He took the binoculars and examined his surroundings.

Toward the north the coast, lit by the sun, curved a little to the left. To the south there was an even more pronounced curve.

His last doubt vanished. It was not a continent, but an island, on which the storm had cast the schooner. And there was no other land in sight. They were on an isolated island. They were lost on the vast Pacific.

The boys took turns at using the binoculars. They did not speak. There was no need for words.

Doniphan was the first to break the silence.

"Come on," he said resolutely. "There's nothing to do but go back."

With a last long look at the expanse of water, the four turned to go.

"Phann, here, Phann!" Service called the dog.

But Phann did not obey. He went snuffling along the wet sand on some quest of his own. Finally he stopped by a small pool and started to lap.

"He's drinking! He's drinking!" Doniphan cried. With one bound he cleared the sand, dipped up some water and tasted it. "Fresh water!" he shouted.

What they saw stretching as far as eye could reach was not the sea. It was a lake.

8

The Cave

Island or continent? The question which was of such vital importance to them was still unanswered. A lake could well be part of an island. If they crossed it and traveled farther they might reach the sea which they had not the means to cross.

On the other hand it was possible, even probable, for a lake of such great size to be situated on a continent.

"Most likely we're in South America," Briant said.

"That's what I've been telling you all along," Doniphan exclaimed. "And it seems I'm right."

"Anyhow, I *did* see water!" Briant could not resist saying.

"Yes, but not the sea."

Briant did not reply. He was too excited by the thought that they might not be prisoners on an island. They would not know for sure, however, until spring, for they could not explore what lay east until then. It was now early April, the beginning of winter in the southern hemisphere.

The west bay, where the schooner had been wrecked, was lashed by blustering wind. They would soon have to leave. Before the end of the month at the latest. Since they had not succeeded in finding a cave nearby, they would have to reconnoiter near the lake which assured them a supply of fresh water. This would take a day or two, and Gordon would worry if they delayed their return that long. Nevertheless Briant suggested that they skirt the lake in a southerly direction. It would save time to do it now they were already there. They had provisions for another forty-eight hours, and the weather promised to remain steady.

There was still another reason why he wanted to push on. The stones across the creek, the shard in the hut, both told of the presence of man. Since nothing pointed to natives in particular, it was quite possible that some other shipwrecked person was, or at least had been, here and perhaps found his way to a town on what might be a continent.

Briant chose the southerly direction because the *Sloughie* lay south. To go north would take them too far afield.

At half-past eight the four set out across the grassy dunes. Phann ran on ahead and pointed coveys of quail which rose with a clatter of wings and settled farther on in the shelter of tall bracken and tufts of wild celery which, the boys decided, could be used for food. They were hungry for some sort of fresh vegetable.

They did not try for the birds because the report of a rifle was still a risk, even though they had no good reason to believe they would run into natives. In the course of the whole ten miles they made that day, they still found no trace of man: no footprints, no smoke, no sail visible on the horizon, no canoe on the water. If this territory had ever been inhabited, it was certainly deserted now.

They did not come across any wild animals, but once or twice they saw what looked like extraordinarily large birds.

"Ostriches!" Service cried.

"Too small for ostriches," Doniphan objected. "But really too big for anything else."

"If they are ostriches," Briant observed, "then we're on a continent."

"Do you really still doubt it?" Doniphan asked.

About seven in the evening they came to a stop. Their way was blocked by one of the rivers which carried the waters of the lake through the countryside. Since they did not want to swim across in the dark, they decided to camp in the open and return to "Sloughie Bay," as they had called it, the following morning.

The crescent moon had set in the Pacific, and the night was bright with stars. Stretched between the massive roots of a huge myrtle whose trunk had a reddish glint, they were soon fast asleep. Only Phann heard the occasional bark of a jackal, or the distant roar of a jaguar or a cougar. His hackles bristled, and he growled softly to himself.

Around four in the morning, when the first gray of dawn showed over the lake, the dog grew restless. He ran here and there, and sniffed the earth as if he'd found a scent.

It was almost seven when Briant woke the others, who were still curled in their blankets. A few biscuits did for breakfast, and then they were on their way.

"Lucky we didn't try to cross the river last night," Wilcox said. "There's a swamp between here and the water. We'd have got stuck."

"That swamp seems to reach so far south you can't see where it ends," Briant said.

"Will you look!" Doniphan exclaimed enthusiastically. "Ducks! Teal! Snipe! If we could only spend the winter here, where there are so many game birds!"

"I don't see why we shouldn't!" Briant remarked thoughtfully.

Behind him was a cliff, the end of a range which formed

almost a right angle. One side faced the bank of the river, the other the lake. It was impossible to tell whether this stone buttress was an extension of that which surrounded Sloughie Bay. It would take further exploring to tell.

The right bank of the river, about twenty feet wide, ran parallel to the stone-range. The low left bank merged with the marshy plain, full of holes and pools, which stretched south clear to the horizon. To discover which way the river flowed, one would have to climb the cliff. Briant decided not to start back without doing this, but first he wanted to examine the point where the river flowed out from the lake.

"Look, everybody!" Wilcox cried before Briant could get started.

What had attracted his attention was a small break-water, little more than piled-up stones, jutting into the river.

"This makes it quite clear," Briant declared. "There *was* somebody here."

"Not a doubt," Doniphan agreed and pointed to pieces of mouldering wood at the end of the breakwater. They were clearly the remains of a hull and one, which must have been part of a post, half-rotted and green with moss, still bore a rusty iron ring.

They stood stock-still and stared at it, and then looked around, as if the man who had put the stones together and had used the boat, must still be within hailing distance.

There was no one. Years had passed since whoever it was had left his traces by the river. Perhaps he had lived and died on this soil without having been able to return to his own country.

Troubled by such thoughts, the boys had not a word to say, but Phann began to behave in a most peculiar manner.

He pricked up his ears, wagged his tail furiously, and sniffed the ground, poking his nose under the tall grass.

"This time he's scented something for sure," Doniphan declared.

The dog paused, lifted one paw, and thrust his head forward. Then he made for a group of trees at the foot of the range.

The boys ran after him. A few moments later they stopped in front of a towering beech. The smooth, gray bark bore man-made marks. Deeply carved into it were initials and a date:

F. B.

1807

Briant, Doniphan, Wilcox, and Service studied the inscription while Phann raced off in great excitement. He barked as if he wanted to urge them to follow him.

"We'll go, but let's keep together," Briant said. It had occurred to him that natives might, after all, be at hand. If they belonged to those tribes of fierce Indians who inhabit South America, their presence would be cause for alarm rather than for relief.

Rifles loaded, pistols held in readiness, the boys advanced. They had not gone twenty steps when Doniphan stooped and picked something up. It was a pickax. The handle had all but rotted away. There was just enough of it left to see that it was not one of the crude tools made by Polynesian savages. It had been produced in Europe or America. Like the ring on the post, the metal was rusted by years of disuse.

A little farther along they detected a patch of yams. Once they must have been planted and tended. Now they had run wild. As the boys looked about for other traces of cultivation, Phann's barks suddenly changed to mournful howls. He ran back to his masters, and lunged forward again.

"He's trying to lead us somewhere," Doniphan said.

A few yards, and the dog stopped in front of a tangled mass of underbrush. In it might be the body of some animal, or even of the man whose trail Phann had found.

When Briant pushed aside the tough branches he saw a narrow opening.

"It's a cave!" he exclaimed, backing a little.

"Could be," Doniphan said. "The question is: What's inside?"

"We'll find out." Briant hacked at the bush with his hatchet and put his ear to the opening. There was no sound.

"I'll go in," Service offered eagerly.

"Watch what Phann does first," Briant advised. But the dog made no attempt to enter. He lifted his head and gave vent to a bloodcurdling howl.

"No use waiting for him," Service said impatiently.

"Just wait until I find out whether there's enough oxygen in there." Briant thrust in a handful of dry grass and set a match to it. The grass burned brightly. It would be possible to breathe in the cave.

"Now let's go!" Service urged.

"At least let's have a light!" Briant cut a resinous branch from one of the pines along the river and lit it, so they could see their way. Then they went in.

The opening was only about five feet high and two across, but widened almost at once to a large, vaulted chamber. The bottom was covered with very fine, dry sand.

Wilcox who had run ahead, stumbled against a stool. It stood in front of a table on which there were household utensils: a stone pitcher, large shells which must have served as plates, and a corroded knife.

Near the wall was a chest knocked together of boards. It contained clothing—mere rags and tatters.

Someone had lived in the cave. But who? And when?

They explored further. In a corner they found a pallet covered with a torn blanket. The boys shrank from touching it for fear of what they might find underneath.

Finally Briant overcame his reluctance. He lifted the cover . . .

The pallet was empty.

A moment later they rejoined Phann outside. He was still howling. As they came up with him they stopped, nailed to the spot with horror.

Between the roots of a tree the crumbling bones of a skeleton littered the ground.

The man who had lived in the cave, perhaps for many years, had come here to die.

9

The Map

Briant, Doniphan, Wilcox, and Service looked at the pile of bones in awed silence. Even when they returned to the cave they still did not speak. Their minds were brim-full of questions to which there were no answers.

Who was this man? Of what nationality? Had he been young at the time he was wrecked? Had he died old? Why hadn't he tried to reach some town or village? Was it too far? Were the difficulties too great? If he hadn't been able to get away, would they?

"Let's go back in," Briant said finally. "We'll make a thorough search, and perhaps we'll find something that will tell us about him. Besides, this cave might turn out to be just the winter shelter we're looking for!"

They lit a second resinous branch, but Phann ran ahead in the dark. He stopped howling and began to sniff at everything in sight.

The first thing they discovered on a shelf fixed to the wall was a bundle of crude candles made of grease, and with a towwick. They set a match to one and put it into a wooden holder which they found close by. This was better than the branch!

What they saw was a good-sized cave. It was quite dry, though the only way air could enter was by the opening through which they had come. There was no moisture on the walls, no drops of the sort one finds in caves of porphyry or basalt, where they form stalactites. These walls were of limestone. The whole place was rather dim, but since limestone is easy to work, they decided they could cut through it and so make a second, and even a third opening.

"If we have to stay longer than five or six months," Wilcox said, "I suppose we could sound out the walls and find one which gives on to another cave. This one isn't really large enough for sleeping and eating and cooking."

"I should say it's about thirty feet long and twenty wide," Service estimated.

"To cut through a wall we'd have to wait till summer, anyway," Briant said. "Let's see what there actually is here."

There was little enough! Evidently the man had been

able to salvage almost nothing. With the wood of the
wreck he had made the table, stools, a bench, a chest, and
a pallet. He had a few tools: a hammer, pickax, hatchet,
chisel, and saw, and some kitchen utensils. There was also
a small keg which, from the smell of it, must have contained brandy.

"We're a lot better off than he was!" Doniphan exclaimed, and everyone felt more confident. "Just think of
all the tools and things on the *Sloughie!*"

And still there was nothing to indicate who the man
had been, and how long he had been dead. Many, many
years, to judge by the crumbling state of the bones, the
rust on the pickax and on the iron ring they had found
by the river. Then, too, it must have taken a long time
for the underbrush to grow so thick at the mouth of the
cave.

They continued their search and found a knife with
broken blades, a compass, a long, pointed marlinespike, a
small winch, and a kettle. No binoculars, and neither rifle
nor pistol. Since the man had nothing to shoot with, he
must have used snares and traps to provide himself with
food.

"What's this?" Service asked, picking up two round
stones.

"Looks like stone balls for that game you showed us
how to play, Briant," Wilcox said. "What did you call it
in French?"

"*Jeu de boules,*" Briant answered. "But I think these
stones are for something different. They're *bolas.* You
connect them with a long cord. South American Indians throw them, and they tangle the legs of animals so
that they can't run away. I read about it somewhere."

"Sounds all right," Service said. "And here's a lasso made of leather."

"You work it like the bolas, only at a shorter distance, I guess," Briant said.

"Do you suppose he was a sailor or an officer?" Doniphan wondered.

"You can't tell from what we've found up to now," Wilcox said and added quickly: "How about this though!"

He pointed to the head of the pallet. A watch hung on a nail fixed in the wall.

"That's not a sailor's watch," Service said. "It's wrought silver, and it has two lids. Here's the key. It's attached to it."

"What time does it show?" Wilcox asked eagerly.

"We have to get it open to see," Briant said. "But it won't tell us anything. It probably stopped days before the man died."

The hinges were oxydized and stuck. When they finally prised open the lid, the hands showed that the watch had stopped at twenty-seven minutes past three. They went to work on the back lid, and there they found something more interesting: the name of the manufacturer and his address. It was *Delpeuch, Saint Malo.*

"Why, that man was French—like me," Briant said softly.

Doniphan, who had been prowling round on his own, held up a notebook. The pages, yellowed with age, bore writing in pencil. It was all but illegible; the name on the top could only just be deciphered. It was *François Baudoin* —F.B., the initials they had seen on the tree.

"He was French all right," Doniphan agreed. "And this must be his journal. What a shame we can't make it out. All but a few words here and there."

"Here's another name," Briant said excitedly. *"Duguay-Trouin.* That must be the name of the ship he was on. And here's a date. The same we found on the tree. The date of the wreck! Fifty-three years ago."

"And no one came to his rescue—ever," Service said soberly.

"Let's all have a look at that journal," Wilcox said rather loudly to take everyone's mind off this solemn truth.

As Doniphan handed over the notebook something fell from between the pages, a piece of folded paper. He opened it. It was a map, and the lines were firm and clear. They had been drawn with ink, probably homemade of soot and water.

"No sailor ever made that map!" Doniphan cried with conviction. "François Baudoin must have been an officer."

"It's a map of where we are," Briant said and tried to control a wild spurt of hope.

They laid it flat on the table and pored over it. There was Sloughie Bay, the cove where they camped. There was the range, the three tiny islands Briant had taken for ships, the forests, the lake . . . On the farther shore were more forests. They extended to another shore, and that shore was washed by the sea.

The boys looked at one another. Their question was answered at long last. They were not on a continent. They were on an island, an island which François Baudoin had not been able to leave!

The boys were as silent as when they had stood beside the heap of bones.

"At least we can get an idea of what we're up against," Doniphan said calmly.

The island was oblong and looked like an enormous

butterfly with spread wings. In the middle of extensive forest land was the lake, about eighteen miles long and five wide. The only elevation was the range which slanted to the north cape where Briant had gone alone. The entire northern portion of the island was sandy and barren. On the farther bank of the river a huge swamp stretched south. Northeast and southeast were dunes which made these parts of the coast very different from Sloughie Bay.

At the foot of the map were figures. According to them the island was about fifty miles long from north to south, at its longest part, and twenty-five at its widest, from west to east. Taking into consideration the irregularities of out-line, the circumference could be estimated at about one hundred and fifty miles.

There was no evidence that it belonged to a group of Polynesian islands, nor that it was an isolated island in the Pacific. However that might be, it was quite clear to the boys that their stay would not be temporary, and that it might well not be brief.

Under these conditions, they decided the cave would make an excellent place to live in, and that they must get all their provisions and equipment there before the winter storms began. Since the map showed that the river emptied into Sloughie Bay, it might be possible to haul their stuff by water on a raft drawn by a rope, or managed by boat hooks.

The main thing now was to return to camp as soon as possible. That very morning. Briant, who had been study-ing the map, pointed out that it would not be necessary to cross the range again. All they had to do was follow the right bank of the river which ran from east to west. That way it would be no more than seven miles.

By common consent the boys resolved to bury the

remains of François Baudoin before they left. They dug
a grave under the tree on which he had carved his initials.
Then they stuffed the mouth of the cave with branches
and briars to keep out animals, and started on the journey
back.

At first the route they had chosen was clear, but toward
four in the afternoon they had to abandon the river bank
because of a long stretch of bog they could not cross
without taking too great a risk. They had to strike off
into the forest.

Briant led, compass in hand, but the thorny thickets and
the massive roots they stumbled over in the twilight of the
heavy foliage, slowed them up, so that the sun had set
before they reached the open. It grew darker and darker,
and still they forged ahead until, around seven in the
evening, they realized they must have lost their way.

"We'll have to spend the night here," Doniphan said.

"Gordon will be terribly worried," Briant objected.
"Besides, we've eaten all the food we took with us because
we expected to be back by now. If we continue west,
we're bound to arrive at our camp."

"If the map isn't wrong!" Doniphan said.

"Why shouldn't the map be right?" Briant asked.

"Why should it!"

Since the boys had already verified the correctness of
the map by the part of the country they knew, Doniphan's
doubts were unjustified, but Briant considered it useless
to enter into an argument and walked on.

At eight, however, they were still in the forest. The
darkness made it impossible to orient themselves. They
stopped, discouraged.

Suddenly, through an opening in the trees, they saw a
bright light that seemed to be traveling through space.

"What is it?" Service exclaimed.

"A meteor, I suppose," Wilcox answered tiredly.

"No, it's a flare!" Briant announced. "A flare launched from the *Sloughie*."

"Then it's a signal from Gordon!" Doniphan cried, and fired a shot in reply.

When the second flare went up, they took their direction by a star from its point of departure. Forty minutes or so later they arrived at their camp.

"That was a wonderful idea, Gordon," Briant said.

"I was afraid you'd lost your way, and so I gave you the position of the schooner."

And then the Elbees rushed up and threw themselves at the explorers. Phann came in for his share of the welcome and swelled the noise with loud barks of joy.

10

Journey to French Den

That night the boys were too exhausted to answer questions: whether they'd seen natives, whether jaguars had attacked them, whether . . .

"We're on an island," was all Briant said, and this time no one contradicted him.

The next morning—it was the fifth of April—the older group: Gordon, Briant, Doniphan, Cross, Wilcox, Service, Webb, Garnett, and Moko, who had given proof of good sense and resourcefulness, met in the bow of the schooner before the Elbees were up.

Briant and Doniphan took turns giving a detailed account of their discoveries. When, in the end, they produced the map, one glance was enough to show that they were, indeed, on an island and that the only possible rescue would have to come from without.

Gordon was, perhaps, less downcast than the others. He had no real home in New Zealand, and his guardian did his duty by the boy rather than give him much personal attention or affection. The young American was a born organizer. He had grown up with tales of pioneering, and the idea of founding a colony in an uninhabited island had nothing frightening for him. He regarded it as an opportunity in line with his own interests and abilities, and soon convinced his companions that life, under these conditions, would not only be bearable, it could be fun! Their spirits rose.

Since, according to Baudoin's map, the island was so large, they tried to find it in Stieler's atlas, but could discover no such sizable region beyond the archipelagoes. Had the island been part of one of these, surely François Baudoin could have crossed one of the narrow separating channels.

"We'll have to move to the cave before winter," Briant said as he shut the book.

"Is it big enough to hold all of us?" Baxter inquired.

"No," Doniphan replied. "But we can break through a wall and enlarge it. We do have tools, after all . . ."

"To begin with, let's use it as it is," Gordon said. "Even if it is close quarters."

"Yes, especially as we have to get there as soon as we can," Briant agreed. "One good storm and the *Sloughie* will fall apart."

"Where will we stay while we're dismantling her?" Doniphan asked.

"In a tent," Gordon said. "We can set one up between the trees on the bank of the river."

"Good idea," Webb seconded him. "Since we're going to take everything to the cave by raft, the nearer the river we are, the better."

"We shouldn't just be calling it the 'cave,'" Garnett said. "Now that it's going to be our home, let's give it a name."

"How about 'French Den?'" Gordon suggested, with a glance at Briant. "In honor of François Baudoin."

And French Den it was.

Putting up the tent did not prove too difficult. By means of spars they connected the stout lower branches of two enormous beeches with a third. This made a solid support for the spare mainsail which they lashed to the ground.

Since they could not begin building the raft from the planking and beams of the *Sloughie* until the schooner was dismantled, they removed provisions, ammunition, and utensils for everyday use at once. The dry weather held, and by the fifteenth of April everything had been taken off except heavy objects, such as the windlass, lead ballast, shrouds, backstays, chains, anchor, and the large supply of lines and cordage.

While the work went on, Doniphan, Wilcox, and Webb took off just enough time to shoot pigeons for the daily meat supply. With so much to do there was hardly an hour to spare. The Elbees went on with their clam digging and hunting for other edible shells, and got themselves thoroughly soaked more than once. Jack joined them, but Briant never heard him laugh and shout along with the rest.

There was every reason to hurry. It got colder day by
day. The early morning temperature was down to freezing.
They took to warmer clothing, and Briant saw to it that
the Elbees did not run around with wet feet. At the first
sign of a cold he made them stay in, close to the fire,
which was kept going day and night. Moko rose to the
occasion by making hot soup and tea for them.

The night of the twenty-fifth a storm the boys would
have dreaded had they still been sleeping on the *Sloughie*,
helped them with their work of demolition. Inside the
tent, which held firm thanks to the trees to which it was
moored, they heard the boom of thunder and saw flashes
of lightning. When they went out in the morning, the
beach was littered with planks, plates of copper with
which the hull had been lined, and pieces of iron. Instead
of having to pry off all this with a great deal of trouble
and toil, they had now only to collect the wreckage and
carry it to the bank. Boy after boy, and often two or
three working together, staggered under heavy loads until
it occurred to Baxter to use spars as levers to lift the
windlass and the stove, for instance, and round blocks of
wood to roll them to their destination.

When the time came to build a raft strong enough to
carry all their equipment, the boys silently longed for
someone with experience to give advice. And then Baxter
suddenly came to the fore as a very important member of
the group. His knowledge of mechanics and his skill in
building and contriving helpful gadgets, were a godsend
at every turn.

His first excellent suggestion was to construct the raft on
the water so they would not have the job of launching it.

"That isn't going to be easy," Doniphan said doubtfully.

"Easier in the long run," Gordon answered.

The beams of the schooner, the keel split in two, the mizzenmast, and the bowsprit were taken to the bank at low tide. As the tide rose and swept these materials into the water, they managed to lash them together to form a crude but solid base for their further work. It was about thirty feet long and half as wide. Briant took the precaution to secure it to a tree so that the tide wouldn't carry it off by night.

On this rough foundation they constructed a platform of planks, nailed together and reinforced with lines. It took three days of hard work with everyone putting forth the utmost effort. There was every reason to hurry, for often, at dawn, they saw that the reeds and the grass were thinly coated with ice.

"We ought to make our getaway before the sixth of May," Briant said.

"Why?" Gordon asked.

"Because the day after tomorrow is new moon, and for the next few days the tide will rise higher. The higher the tide, the easier for our raft to ride. Just think what a job it would be if we had to push it or haul it!"

"That's true," Gordon said. "We'll leave in three days at the latest."

Everyone agreed and took as brief rests as possible to speed the work.

On the third of May they began to load, taking care to distribute the weight evenly. Jenkins, Iverson, Dole, and Costar carried small objects: instruments, cooking utensils, and books, while the older boys took care of the rest, including the tinned goods and the sacks of salt they had wisely collected from the rocks that jutted into the bay.

It would have taken more than their combined strength to lift the stove, the iron bindings, and the copper plates

from bank to platform. Fortunately Baxter was able to rig
a crane with planks and ropes. He worked it with the
help of the winch and was able to deposit considerable
loads gradually and with scarcely a bump.

By the fifth, each object was in place. There was nothing to do but loose the line to free the raft to float.

"One more thing," Gordon said. "From where we're
going we won't be able to watch the sea, and if a ship did
pass this way, we'd not know it and so we'd not be able
to signal. I think we ought to put up the mast by the
range and hoist one of our flags."

This was at once accepted by all, even though it meant
another bout of work at a time when they were very tired.

When the mast had been firmly dug into the ground,
Baxter hoisted the English flag which Doniphan immediately saluted with a shot.

"Doniphan's taking possession of the island in the name
of Britain," Gordon whispered to Briant.

"I should be very much surprised if it wasn't already
British," Briant whispered back, and Gordon, for once,
scowled. He would have liked to take the island for
America.

The next morning they took down the tent and added
it to the cargo. Moko had seen to it that enough provisions
to last them for a trip of two or three days would be
within easy reach. At half past eight they went on board,
armed with boathooks and spars to steer their craft.

Shortly before nine the tide started rising. The raft
shook and creaked, but the heavy objects, all of which
had been lashed in place, stood firm.

"Ready!" Briant called.

"Ready!" Doniphan and Baxter echoed.

The line was loosed.

"Here we go!" Wilcox sang out.

They were moving. It had worked. Dragging the yawl in its wake, the raft was traveling on the river. The boys felt a rush of pride. After all, they had done it all themselves!

They tried to keep the raft as close to the right bank as possible. It floated smoothly, but slowly. They took two hours to make a mile. According to Briant's estimate the river measured six miles from Sloughie Bay to French Den. Since they could not count on making more than two miles at high tide, it would take several tide-periods to bring them to the cave.

"What's more," Gordon said, "I think we'd better not take advantage of the night tide. We can't see to steer in the dark, and a shock might tear the raft apart."

This meant a delay of twenty-four hours, but it was better than endangering their precious load. The time passed quickly. Doniphan had brought down a brace of partridges and two fat young bustards, game birds related to plovers, which made an excellent supper.

Baxter, Webb, and Cross took turns watching by night. Apart from the fact that it grew very cold, nothing happened to cause them alarm. The cold in itself was bad enough! What if the lake had already frozen over, and the sun cracked this first ice! Blocks floating down the river might collide with the raft.

The boys were much concerned about this possibility, yet they could not hurry the raft.

Toward one in the afternoon they reached the swampy region Briant had seen before, and decided to explore it briefly. Doniphan and Wilcox took the yawl, navigated by Moko, and went a mile or so north. To their great satisfaction they came across many water birds and were able to provide snipe for a first meal in French Den.

The second night was so ice-cold that the Elbees whimpered at having had to leave the camp near the *Sloughie,* and even Briant could hardly comfort them.

At last, by afternoon of the next day, the tide which held until half past three in the afternoon, swept them towards the lake. To shrieks of joy from the Elbees, they landed on the bank opposite French Den.

II

Settling in for the Winter

Dole frisked and leaped about like a puppy. Iverson and Jenkins ran along the shore, but Costar stood still, signaled to Moko and, when he had him to himself, asked: "Are we going to have a good lunch?"

"Just corned-beef and a few biscuits. It takes time to cook snipe. You may be sure you'll have a first-rate sup-per." And Moko showed his splendid teeth in a broad grin.

Costar gave him a friendly punch in the ribs, and joined the rest. The Elbees had orders not to go so far that they'd be out of sight.

"Why aren't you with them?" Briant asked his brother.

"I'd rather stay here."

"You don't take enough exercise. I'm worried about you, Jack. You're hiding something. Believe me, I wouldn't pry into your business if I didn't see you're unhappy. I'd like to help."

"Thanks, but I'm perfectly all right."

Always the same sort of unsatisfactory answer! Briant was determined to get to the bottom of the mystery as soon as the first press of work was over. He had no time now. If they wanted to spend that night in French Den, there was plenty to do.

As soon as the raft had been moored, those of the boys who did not yet know the cave, were led in, headed by Moko with a ship's lantern which gave far more light than candles.

The branches across the entrance had not been disturbed. Neither man nor animal had tried to get in. One by one they slipped through the narrow opening.

"It's going to be tight quarters," Baxter said. "Just as we thought."

"Maybe we can make a framework and arrange the pallets one on top of the other like berths in a cabin," Garnett suggested.

"What for?" Wilcox asked. "When there's room to put them down in a row?"

"Because then there won't be room to move around," Webb objected.

"Well, then we won't move around. Have you something better to offer, Webb?" Briant asked rather crossly.

"No, but . . ."

"No buts," Service declared. "The important thing is that we have a place to stay. After all, we can't expect an apartment with livingroom, diningroom, bedroom, kitchen, and bath."

"Of course not," Cross said. "There should at least be a kitchen, though."

"I could cook outside," Moko offered.

"Not in bad weather," Briant said. "I think that, by tomorrow, we'll have the stove in the cave."

"The stove! In the place where we're going to eat and sleep!" Doniphan exclaimed indignantly.

"Poor Lord Doniphan," Service jeered. "He'll have to breathe cooking fumes. Won't that be just too bad."

"If I choose to, Mr. Assistant Cook," Doniphan replied haughtily.

"Oh, come," Gordon broke in on what threatened to grow beyond good-natured banter. "Whether we like it or not, we'll have to stand it for a while. The stove, incidentally, will give heat, too. That's an advantage. And by and by we'll try to break through a wall and enlarge the cave. For now we'll have to take it as it is."

While the boys put down the pallets, Moko collected big stones for an outdoor fireplace. Wilcox and Webb looked for wood and soon brought a bundle of dry branches. In a short time they had a fire going, and toward six soup, made of bouillon cubes, was ready.

They had to wait for the main dish: ducks and snipe on a spit, which Dole and Iverson kept turning. Costar would have liked to dunk a biscuit in the drip-pan below, but didn't want to seem too greedy with everyone watching. Phann showed signs of deep interest and licked his chops.

By seven o'clock they sat round the table from the *Sloughie* and ate heartily after the makeshift meals of the last few days.

They were very tired, but before going to bed they paid a visit to the grave of François Baudoin whose home they now occupied. The last sun-rays had paled, and the lake was already touched with darkness.

The next morning, the ninth of May, and for three days after, they were busy unloading the raft, a task which needed all hands. They were working against time, for the mornings were gray and foggy and this, together with the increasing cold, meant rain and, maybe, snow. Even the hunters were commandeered for hauling, but the water fowl were so abundant that a quarter of an hour here and there was enough to shoot pintail ducks and teal. Gordon was worried about wasting ammunition. He had listed what there was and, though the supply was still plentiful, he begged them to be sparing with it.

"It's in your own interest," he told them. "We have to think of the future."

"And we have to eat in the present," Doniphan countered. "Besides, we agreed to save on the tinned goods to make them last as long as possible. We'll need them when we get a chance to leave the island."

"Leave the island!" Gordon exclaimed. "What makes you think we'll be able to build a boat that could sail the sea!"

"Why shouldn't we! Especially if there's a continent close by. In any case, I can tell you I'm not anxious to die on this island like Briant's fellow Frenchman."

"We all want to live," Gordon said cheerfully. "And before thinking of leaving, we have to get used to the idea of living right here, perhaps for years and years."

"That's my Gordon!" Doniphan cried. "Delighted with the idea of founding a colony, I suppose."

"Why not, if we can't do otherwise."

"I don't think you'll get up much enthusiasm for it, not even from your friend Briant."

"There'll be lots of time to discuss all this," Gordon said peaceably. "As for Briant . . ." he lowered his voice.

"You're being very unfair to him. He's a good fellow and has given us proof of his courage and unselfishness."

"You're making a hero out of him. I guess you think he's perfect."

"Nobody's perfect. But the way you're acting might lead to splitting our forces. That would be a bad business for all of us. So please stop finding fault with Briant. Everybody likes him."

"Everybody?"

"Most of us, anyway. I can't understand what you, Wilcox, Cross, and Webb have against him. Please, Doniphan, think it over."

"I already have."

Gordon gave up. He saw that Doniphan turned a deaf ear to his warning, and foresaw trouble.

On the thirteenth the unloading job was completed. The stove had been installed and Baxter had managed to make a hole in the wall for the pipe which was to carry the smoke outside. Moko declared that it worked and that they could cook indoors in bad weather.

The heavy equipment which would not fit into the cave, was stacked against a huge boulder and covered with tarpaulin from the schooner.

During the week that followed Doniphan, Webb, Wilcox, and Cross, accompanied by Garnett and Service, satisfied their taste for hunting to the full. On one of their expeditions they found a number of traps. They were deep trenches covered over with branches. François Baudoin must have laid them. One of them contained the bones of some creature, but they could not tell what it was.

Wilcox let himself down and retrieved the bones.

"It was big," he said. "And a quadruped. Here are the bones of four feet."

"Might have been five-footed, a freak sheep or something."

"That isn't even funny, Service," Cross said.

"We'll do you a favor and laugh just the same," Garnett said easily.

Doniphan had been examining the bones.

"Look at the size of the skull and those teeth still in the jaw!"

"Do you suppose it was a lion or a tiger?" Cross asked nervously.

"No, but maybe a cougar or a jaguar. Both dangerous!"

"We'll have to be careful," Webb warned.

"And not go off too far," Cross added.

"Did you hear that, Phann?" Service addressed the dog. "There are big, bad animals here."

Phann barked cheerfully.

"Let's set the traps again," Wilcox suggested. "How about cutting some fresh branches to put over them?"

"If you like," Doniphan said grudgingly. "I, for my part, prefer shooting animals when they're at large, and not killing them in a pit where they can't defend themselves."

"We'll save bullets this way."

The rest agreed and proceeded to cut branches thick with leaves, and lay them across the openings. When Wilcox had notched a number of trees so that they would find the place again, they returned to French Den.

For days they looked for results in their traps, but in vain. In the meantime Briant and Gordon made two discoveries, unexciting, yet important for their larder. For one thing they caught trout and pike in the lake. For another, they found the wild celery Briant had noticed on the first trip, and also cress which, so Gordon said, would keep them from getting scurvy. Thus a gap in their diet was filled.

And then, one morning, when Briant, Gordon, and Doniphan had set out to look for another cave in which they might perhaps stow the bulkier objects of the *Sloughie*, they heard hoarse cries from one of the traps.

Briant started towards it, but Doniphan raced ahead. When they were about twenty feet away, the sound grew louder. Phann's ears were up and his tail out straight behind.

There was a large breach in the branches and the earth was grooved deeply where something big had slid down.

"Here, Phann, here!" Doniphan cried. Phann ran up to him and barked, but with no sign of alarm.

Briant and Doniphan peered down.

"Come and look!" they called.

"It's not a jaguar, is it?" Webb inquired.

"No," Doniphan said. "Nor a cougar. It's something on two legs. Looks like an ostrich to me."

"It is and it isn't," Gordon decided. "A bit too small for an ostrich. I've seen pictures of this: the head's like that of a goose, and the body has a fleece of short, grayish-white feathers. In fact, it's a nandu."

"Let's take it alive," Wilcox said.

"If we can," Cross said doubtfully.

"I'm going to try." Wilcox lowered himself into the trap at the risk of being bitten. The nandu threshed about furiously, but when the boy threw his blazer over its head it became motionless.

"Throw me a couple of handkerchiefs," he said. "No, I'll need three."

He knotted them together and tied the nandu's legs. Now it was possible to drag him out of the trap.

"Now that we have it, what on earth are we going to do with it?" Cross asked.

"I'll tell you," said Service, who never had any doubts about anything. "We'll take it to French Den, tame it, and train it for a mount. Don't you remember how Jack, in *The Swiss Family Robinson*, rode the ostrich?"

When they reached French Den with their find, the Elbees went wild with excitement. The creature was released from its bonds and tied to a tree by a long cord.

"Are you really going to ride it? Can I come too?" Costar asked eagerly.

"If you're good," Service teased.

"I'll be the best ever."

"And you think you'll dare to get on its back?"

"If you let me hold on to you. I'll ride behind you."

"And how about the time you were scared to death to ride on the tortoise?"

"That was different," Costar defended himself. "The tortoise tried to drag me into the water."

"And maybe this bird will take you up into the air," Service said.

At this Costar grew very quiet and seemed to be thinking over the matter.

That evening Gordon called a meeting of the older boys.

"The Elbees haven't enough to do," he said. "Soon they won't even be able to be out much. They can help with little things, but they'll have too much time on their hands. I think we ought to make a sort of program for the day. Why don't we teach them, so they'll have their lessons just as if they were at Chairman School?"

"There are some books," Briant said. "And we can teach them what we've learned ourselves."

"Yes, we remember a lot, I'm sure," Service said.

"And it'll freshen it up for us," Wilcox added. "So when we get back we won't have lost so much time."

So a schedule was worked out and rigidly kept. And a good thing it was, for there were days on end when the Elbees could only go outside for minutes.

The one thing that grew more and more annoying was the inconvenience of such small quarters. The problem of enlarging the cave had become pressing.

12

Chairman Island

Had the cave been of granite, their tools would have been useless. Limestone offered no difficulties. When they made the opening for the stovepipe they had found out that a pick or a pickax was enough for the job.

Now, before starting on their big project, they experimented further on the limestone by widening the entrance to the cave so that they could fit into it one of the doors of the *Sloughie,* and by piercing the wall on either side to let in light and air.

On the twenty-seventh of May, they were ready to begin enlarging.

"If we cut through at a slant," Briant proposed, "we might come out on the lake side. That would give us a second entrance to French Den, so when the snow piles up at one, we'd still have the other."

"I don't think there are more than forty to fifty feet of stone between our room and the east," Baxter said. "We can take our direction by compass. How about first making a shaft, though? There'd be less danger of caving-in and later, when we've hollowed out a second room, the shaft could serve as a passage running between."

This plan was accepted, especially as it would give them a chance to observe whether water came through as they worked.

They did not have to make much of an effort. The stone could have almost been cut with a knife! Debris was immediately removed and, as the shaft grew, they reinforced the sides with slabs of wood salvaged from the partitions of the schooner.

Since, for want of space, only two or three could work at a time, the others took apart the raft and hauled planks, beams, and lines to the shelter of the boulder where they had stored other heavy objects.

They had been at it for three days. The shaft was already four or five feet long when Briant, bent over his pick like a miner, heard a dull noise which seemed to come from the inside of the mass of rock. He straightened and listened, then put his ear to the wall. Again he heard the sound.

He called to Gordon and Baxter who were working nearer the room.

"You're imagining it," Gordon said. "You just thought you heard something."

"Stand where I did," Briant replied. "And then put your ear to the wall and listen."

Gordon entered the shaft and came out a minute later.

"You're right. I heard something, too. It was like a muffled growl."

Baxter went in next.

"Whatever can it be?" he asked.

"I don't know," Gordon said. "But I think we should tell Doniphan and the others."

"Not the Elbees," Briant said quickly. "They'd be scared to death."

Since it was dinner time, the younger boys had just come in and overheard his last words. They looked at him with frightened eyes.

Doniphan, Wilcox, Webb, and Garnett took turns entering the shaft and listening. Evidently the noise had stopped, for as one after the other emerged, they declared Gordon and Briant must have been mistaken.

"We're not, but we'll go on with the work just the same," Gordon said quietly.

Nothing disturbed them during their meal, but towards nine the sounds came again. This time they were quite distinct. Phann bounded into the shaft. When he returned his hackles were up, and his teeth bared. He started barking viciously.

"We've got to get the Elbees to bed," Briant whispered to Gordon.

Dole, Costar, and even Jenkins and Iverson could not hide their terror. They were young enough to still believe in the gnomes and giants of the fairy tales they had been told and, what was worse, in ghosts that might haunt the cave. The fact that Phann was showing every sign of uneasiness increased their alarm. But the sounds had stopped, and finally everyone went to bed except Briant and Moko who took turns on watch.

The next morning they all rose early. Everything was quiet, and the dog behaved normally.

"Perhaps those sounds didn't come from an animal," Doniphan said. "Might be a spring bubbling up somewhere inside."

"If it were a spring, you'd hear it all the time," Wilcox objected.

"I think it may be wind howling through some crack we don't know of," Gordon said.

"Let's climb to where we can look down on the top of the cave," Service proposed. "Then we might be able to see the crack."

In a few minutes he and the others were on the plateau above French Den. The rocks were so covered with short, thick grass that they could see nothing at all.

They decided to go on with their excavating. There was no more noise, but Baxter made a curious discovery: the wall which, up to then, had given out a dull sound, now rang under the pick as if there were a cavity beyond.

During supper they discussed this with eager excitement. If there was another natural cave it would save them an enormous amount of work.

So intent were they on this question that it was not till the end of their meal that Gordon noticed Phann was not there. It was unheard-of for the dog to be absent when eating was going on. They called, but he did not come. They looked out of the door. He was nowhere in sight.

Gordon and Doniphan ran, one toward the river, the other to the lake. There was no trace of the dog. He couldn't have lost his way and he would certainly have come at Gordon's call if he were anywhere within earshot.

After an hour of vain search the boys finally gave up and went to bed. Gordon remained seated at the table and

Briant stayed up with him. They could not sleep. The thought of having lost Phann made them feel lonely and somehow farther away from home.

Suddenly the silence was broken, this time by snarls and yelps of pain which grew louder by the minute.

"It's there by the shaft," Briant cried.

By this time everybody was awake. They ran to the opening and listened, and Briant went into the shaft.

"There must be a second cave," he said. "With an entrance at the foot of the cliffs."

"A cave where animals come to spend the night," Gordon added.

"We can't do anything before daylight," Doniphan said sensibly.

Hardly were the words out of his mouth when a volley of barks exploded from beyond the shaft.

"That's Phann!" Gordon cried. "And he's fighting!"

Minutes later all was still, yet Phann did not return. He could have been hurt, badly hurt, and no one could get to him!

"It's positive there's another cave," Baxter said. "The entrance must be hidden under ferns and underbrush. We'll look at dawn."

But when they searched the next morning, they still found nothing, and Phann did not reappear.

With heavy hearts they went on with their work and advanced the shaft another two feet. From time to time, one or another put his ear to the wall, but no one reported the slightest sound. After lunch they proceeded more cautiously, for if a pick suddenly struck through, it was quite possible that a jaguar, or a cougar might leap at the opening and attack them. Since there was danger, the

Elbees were told to go and play on the shore. Doniphan, Wilcox, and Webb stood ready to help, pistols in hand.

Towards two o'clock Briant uttered a cry. His pick had broken through. Stone crumbled and fell. He faced a large gap.

Before he could retreat, something crowded out and grazed his legs. The next instant Phann rushed into the cave.

The first thing he did was to go to his bowl of water and lap thirstily. Then he jumped joyfully on Gordon. He was wagging his tail. His fur lay smooth. So there was nothing to be afraid of.

Briant took a lantern and wriggled through the gap. Gordon, Doniphan, Wilcox, Baxter, and Moko followed. Someone gave a gasp of surprise. They were in a cave with not a gleam of light from the outside. It was about as wide as French Den, but at least fifty feet long. At first they wondered whether it held enough oxygen, but the lantern burned and Phann had, after all, spent a lot of time in there.

As they advanced slowly, Wilcox's foot struck against something. Briant lowered the lantern to see.

"It's a jackal!" Baxter cried. "And he's very dead."

"Thanks to Phann," Briant said.

"So that's the explanation of all that snarling and barking," Gordon added.

"We have to know whether other jackals come to this cave to spend the night," Doniphan declared. "And we have to know before we can even think of using it for quarters of our own."

"Let's go outside and walk around and shout," Baxter suggested. "Some of you stay in here and answer. That way we should soon be able to find out where there's an opening."

They did this and quickly discovered an entrance in the rock. It was covered over with underbrush and half caved-in besides. Either the shock produced by the picks, or Phann's sudden chasing of the jackals, or both, had caused a landslide. That was why, for twenty-four hours, the dog had been forced to remain where he was.

The second cave, with an entrance on the lake, was the talk of the day. The boys immediately dubbed it the "Hall," and began to make it habitable. The opening was enlarged and fitted with a door. Vents for light and air were cut through the stone, and then they could move in. The Hall was to serve as dormitory and study and storeroom for furniture and tins and everything else that required a safe, dry shelter. It was a good two weeks before they had finished, and only just in the nick of time, for winter had come in earnest.

For a time the lake looked like a sea, with great waves thundering on the shore. The yawl had to be dragged ashore for fear it might be carried away. Even the nandu had to be taken inside, at least until they could construct some enclosure for him, protected from wind and cold.

Since the gale blew from the west, it was lucky they now had an east entrance to their cave-home.

"Now that we're settled, we ought to give names to the various parts of the island, so that we don't have to keep saying 'range, east cape,' and all," Webb said.

"Let's choose pretty names," Iverson put in.

"The Robinsons always had names for everything," Service reminded them.

"And that's what we are," Cross said. "Robinsons! Robinson Crusoe times fifteen!"

"We already have two names," Briant said. "Sloughie Bay and French Den."

"Let's call the river 'Zealand River,'" Baxter proposed. "In honor of our country."

"And the lake 'Home Lake,'" Doniphan said. "That'll go for all of us, no matter where we're from."

Other names they agreed on were 'Auckland Hill' for the range, 'False Sea Point' for the cape from which Briant had seen what he took for the sea, 'Trap Woods,' 'Bog Woods,' 'South Moors' for the swamps, 'Wreck Coast' for where the tempest had cast the *Sloughie*, and finally 'Sports Terrace' for the area between river and lake. This lay flat in front of the entrance to the hall and was to be used for sports and exercise.

"How about the whole island?" Doniphan asked. "We haven't named that."

"I know a name," Costar piped up.

"Hear, hear! Little Costar's going to name the island," Garnett said jokingly.

"I'll bet he's going to call it 'Isle of Babes,'" Service teased.

"Let him have his say," Briant said. "Go ahead, Costar. We'd like to hear what name you've found."

"I just thought," Costar said in a small voice, "that since we're all pupils of Chairman School, why not call this island 'Chairman Island?'"

"Chairman Island!" they all chorused and clapped. Costar glowed with pride.

"Now that we have a name for everything, there's one more problem," Briant said. "We need someone to govern our island. A chief."

"What do you mean—chief?" Doniphan said suspiciously.

"Only, that one of us ought to have authority over the others. A country has to be governed. So does Chairman Island."

"A chief! We want a chief!" the Elbees shouted.

"All right, but on condition it's for a limited time," Doniphan said. "Say a year."

"And that he can be re-elected," Briant added.

"Agreed, but who shall it be?" Doniphan asked in a rather anxious tone. He was obviously afraid that the choice might fall on Briant.

"The cleverest of us—Gordon!" Briant stated in a matter-of-fact tone.

"Gordon! Hurrah for Gordon!" They all cried with one accord. Not one voice was lacking.

Gordon looked embarrassed. He felt like refusing this honor because he knew he was better at organizing than at giving orders. Then he thought of the jealousies and quick tempers that might give trouble. He would be in a better position to keep peace if he had authority. So he accepted and became chief of the boys on Chairman Island.

13

Winter in June

In the region around the South Pole winter begins in July, which corresponds to January in the northern zone. In Chairman Island it began in May, and there was no telling how long it would last. If the island lay in a higher latitude than New Zealand, certainly till mid-September, and after that the equinoctial storms had to be reckoned with. It would be October before the boys could undertake trips of any length. For five months they would have to spend most of the time indoors.

Gordon immediately set about making a schedule which would keep them from being bored and restless.

One of the first things he put up to the older group was giving up fagging. Doniphan was not entirely in agreement with him, but realized that, thrown together as they were from morning till night, it would not do to have the younger boys wait on their seniors. No fags on Chairman Island! The Elbees would, of course, be assigned jobs they could manage and which were for the good of all, but no one was to give them orders which involved serving him personally.

Next came the question of teaching those who, at Chairman School, would have been in the lower forms. Since the books in the *Sloughie*'s library were too advanced for them, the older boys took turns giving them lessons in arithmetic, geography, and history. Here Doniphan, with his brilliant mind and lively explanations, easily surpassed all the rest. Had it not been for his haughty manner, especially to those younger than he, he would have been a general favorite.

The older boys had no one to teach them, so they decided to hold what they called "discussions" on some subject chosen from the fields of science, history, or current events. To "discuss" intelligently, they had to read up on whatever they were going to talk about, and so they learned new facts and also how to present them.

Whenever the weather permitted they took exercise.

Both in physical and mental efforts they kept in mind the three rules on which Anglo-Saxon education is based:

1. If you are afraid to do something, do it.

2. Make the greatest effort you are capable of on every possible occasion.

3. Don't give up when you're tired. Fatigue is part of any kind of useful work.

Just to take care of the needs of daily living took a good two hours in the morning and again in the evening. Special tasks were given to individual boys: crossing out days on the calendar, for instance, and winding watches and clocks. When it was decided that they ought to keep a journal and note down everything that happened on Chairman Island, Baxter volunteered for the job. Webb took readings of thermometer and barometer, and noted them down.

One great problem was the laundry. There was so much of it! Everyone got dirty, but especially the Elbees who rolled on Sports Terrace and muddied their clothes when they fished on the shore of the lake. They tried, and even reminded one another to keep clean, but soon forgot all about it. Briant, of course, defended them on the score of their age, but Gordon scolded because he was worried.

Moko, of his own accord, promised to take care of the laundry problem. One person could not possibly cope with it, though, and so the older boys took turns helping. This particular work, needless to say, was little to their liking.

On Sundays they always tried to do something different from on weekdays. The dinner was extra good; they ran races on Sports Terrace, and had music in the evening. Garnett played his accordion and the rest sang, often a bit off pitch, but always with great enthusiasm. Jack, who was the only one with a true and really good voice and had sung solo at school many times, refused to take part in the singing as in everything else.

In June the thermometer dropped to ten degrees above zero. Snow fell for hours in close, heavy flakes. When it stopped they went out to have a snowball fight. Everyone shouted, and dodged, or stooped to scoop up another, and yet another handful of snow. Suddenly Jack gave a smothered cry. A snowball, thrown by Cross, had hit him on the head.

"I didn't do it on purpose," Cross said.

"All the same, you shouldn't have thrown so hard," Briant reproached him.

"Well, if Jack doesn't want to play, why does he stand in the way?"

"Much ado about nothing!" Doniphan jeered.

"You're right about its not being anything serious," Briant said. "All I meant was that Cross should be more careful."

"Why make a fuss when he didn't do it on purpose!"

"I don't see why you're interfering, Doniphan. It's between Cross and me."

"I won't stand for that tone you're taking with me!"

"Very well, Doniphan," Briant said and crossed his arms on his chest. "I'm ready, when and where you please."

Luckily Gordon arrived before they actually got into a fight, but it was clear that, sooner or later, those two would come to blows.

Snowballs had stopped being fun, so they started making an enormous snowman with a long nose and a wide mouth. By day Dole and Costar pelted him with icicles, but when it got dark the white giant looked so much like a bogeyman that they skirted him at a good distance.

The end of June put an end to all such games. The snow

lay four feet deep and made walking more than a few yards from French Den impossible. The bitter cold posed other problems than merely staying in. There were water, heat, and food to think of. Their water supply, lake and river, was frozen over and it was due only to Baxter's ingenuity that they had water. With a pipe from the *Sloughie*, let into the river through a hole in the ice, he set up a very fair connection with the cave.

As for heat and light, they still had oil for the lantern, and a supply of candles to which they added by making new candles from the grease Moko carefully saved from his cooking. But the wood-pile was getting low. They waited for a windless day to go to Trap Woods to replenish it.

The soft snow, which had come waist-high only a few days ago, was now frozen over. So were the lake and the river, so that they could take the shortest cuts they knew. The Elbees scampered ahead and took long slides on the ice, while the woodcutters set to work stripping away the low branches which would flare up and burn for only a few minutes. Then they felled trees which they had chosen for their medium size. While they were wielding their axes all went well, but when they had finished they faced the problem of hauling all this wood to French Den.

It was then Moko had his great idea. They could take the big table, he said. It measured twelve by four feet. If they slid it to the spot upside down, legs in the air, it would make a fine sledge to take their load back.

"Good for you, Moko!" Briant cried.

"Wait and see if his plan works," Doniphan said cautiously.

It did! With four boys harnessed to the makeshift sled, they managed to carry a good load of wood. They made the trip back and forth twice over, and that night they ate so heartily that Gordon worried.

Because of the snow and the cold there were few birds about. Moko had to dig deeper and deeper into the tinned food supply. There were, after all, fifteen mouths to feed. Not counting Phann! The nandu had to be fed, too. Since he was a vegetarian he did not make any important inroads on their stock, but it was not easy to keep him in food. Service, who still counted on riding him, had to scrape under four feet of snow for grass and lichen. The nandu slimmed down considerably, but his master hoped he would get his paunch back by spring. For the rest, the creature never showed any sign of gratitude or affection. It remained wild and unfriendly, and there was doubt whether it would ever be possible to tame it.

To help with the meat supply Wilcox, skilled in all kinds of hunting, made simple wooden traps propped by pieces of wood shaped like a four. These yielded small game. He also made snares by mounting the fishing nets of the *Sloughie* on stakes, and so caught a number of birds, though most of the smaller ones slipped through the meshes.

On the ninth of July, Briant noticed that the wind had veered. It was blowing from the south. The cold was intense.

"I was afraid of this," Gordon said. "I shouldn't wonder if the worst winter months were still ahead."

"That means that the *Sloughie*'s nearer the South Pole than we thought," Briant said.

"And yet our atlas doesn't show a single island in the Antarctic."

"I don't understand it," Briant said impatiently. "And I

don't know in what direction we'll have to go when we leave Chairman Island."

"Leave!" Gordon exclaimed. "So you're still playing with that idea!"

"I've never stopped, Gordon. If we were able to build a boat that's more or less seaworthy, I'd be willing to go alone."

"All right," Gordon said, without going into it further. "Anyhow, there's no hurry. We haven't even entirely organized our little colony."

You forget that we all have countries of our own. Homes . . ."

"No, I don't, Briant. But we're not really unhappy here, are we? Everything's going fine. We have all we need, don't we?"

"Well, not exactly all," Briant said, and stopped talking about leaving the island because he saw that it bothered Gordon. "How about oil, for instance?"

"We can't do anything about that while it's still so cold. Later on we might go after seals."

It got colder and colder. They lived in a white world with crystal trees, and long, thin icicles flashing in the sun. Once they found tracks which were made by neither jackal, cougar, nor jaguar.

"Perhaps wild cats made them," Gordon said.

"Oh, if they're only cats," Costar said in a relieved tone.

"Tigers are cats, too," Jenkins informed him.

"Is that true, Service?" Costar asked. "Can cats be big and fierce, like tigers?"

"They certainly can. They could crunch you as if you were a mouse."

Costar backed away from the tracks and made it his

business to keep close to Service or another of the older boys.

The fifteenth of July was St. Swithin's Day which, as a weather indicator, corresponds to St. Médard's in France.

"If it rains today," Briant said, "it'll rain for forty days running."

"What's the difference?" Garnett said. "Whichever way you look at it, it's a rough season. I wish the summer'd come quickly."

"What St. Swithin's or St. Médard's bring doesn't hold here anyway," Cross said.

There was no rain, but the thermometer dropped. By the first week in August it was seventeen below. Finally, on the sixteenth, the temperature was ten above again. The day was clear and calm. Doniphan, Briant, Service, and Wilcox decided to go to Sloughie Bay. If they set out early, they could be back before night.

They were anxious to go for two reasons. One was to try and find seals, the other to replace the flag on their signal mast. Wind, rain, and snow must have ripped it to tatters long before now.

"We'll put up a new flag," Briant said. "And nail a board with directions to French Den to the mast, so that if a sailor sees the flag and lands, he'll know how to find us."

Since the swamp of Bog Woods was frozen over, they did not have to skirt it. The route they took was so direct it brought them to Sloughie Bay by nine o'clock.

The first thing they saw was a flock of penguins. They stood upright on the reef and uttered harsh, rather disagreeable cries.

"They look like soldiers lined up for review," Service remarked.

"But they're not worth a shot," Baxter said. "No good to eat."

Briant wisely said nothing, for had he agreed with Baxter, Doniphan would certainly have fired on the penguins, just to be contrary. As it was, he let them alone.

A little farther on they saw what they were looking for: seals. They were sporting in the waves, or resting on sandbanks covered with a layer of ice. The moment the boys approached, they plunged into the sea and disappeared. It would take special measures to capture them, and that meant another expedition later on.

After a hasty lunch the boys looked over the bay. White drifts reached all the way from Zealand River to False Sea Point. Besides the penguins, and a few petrels and gulls, there was not a living creature in sight. What was left of the schooner lay hidden under snow. The sea was still empty to the horizon. And hundreds of miles beyond that horizon was New Zealand.

Baxter hoisted the new flag and nailed the board to the mast. It gave the situation of French Den as six miles up the river. They were ready to start back. Their trip had been successful in that they could report that there were seals in Sloughie Bay. They would return and hunt them as soon as the weather permitted.

Already the snow was beginning to melt, and the ice on the lake showed cracks here and there. Winter was slowly coming to an end, and the little colony had not suffered too great hardship. Apart from a cold or two, there had been no illness. Everyone noticed how the Elbees had grown. And they were well up in their studies. The only one who had given trouble was Dole. He was not only often inattentive in class, but tried again and again to shirk his share of the work. When he refused to obey Gordon, chief of Chairman Island, the whole group decided that a whipping was in order.

With everyone watching, Wilcox gave Dole six sharp strokes with a rod. All would-be slackers now knew what was in store for them, and the punishment did not need to be repeated.

This happened on the tenth of September, six months after the *Sloughie* had been wrecked on Chairman Island.

14

The Nandu and Other Animals

There should have been at least a sign of spring by mid-September. Yet all through that month and into October there was no change for the better. Storm after storm broke over the island. Even the severe cold had been easier to bear. Auckland Hill seemed to shake under the gales from the south. Unimpeded they rushed over the flat moors. Whenever the wind let up a little, rain and hail pounded the earth.

Whatever animals there were had disappeared. Either they had gone into hiding, or they had fled to the forests of the interior for shelter. The fish had left the rough surface of the water for the safe calm of the bottom.

To while away the time they were forced to remain indoors, the boys tried to think up a way to haul wood, now that the layer of frozen snow, which had carried the table-sledge, was melting down. Baxter, who was usually on the quiet side but came to life when it was a question of mechanical contrivances, had the best idea. They could use the wheels of the windlass, he said, and make a cart. Since these wheels had notches which could not be smoothed away, he filled the spaces between with wedges whittled out of wood. Then he bound the whole with iron and connected the two wheels by an iron bar. On this foundation they knocked together a wooden platform.

"I wish your nandu could pull a load," Garnett said, when he and Wilcox had unwillingly taken the place of draft animals. "It's the only creature we have around, and good for absolutely nothing."

"Just wait till I ride him," Service defended his so-called "pet."

"Well, I hope it won't be too long a wait. It's a big bother—always trying to break its cord."

Service approached the nandu only to be met by an angry lunge. It bit or kicked anyone who ventured too close.

"What makes you think he'll let you ride him?" Gordon asked with reasonable doubt.

"Jack in *The Swiss Family Robinson* rode his ostrich, so why shouldn't I ride mine?"

"There's a big difference between you and Jack, and between his ostrich and yours," Gordon said.

"What difference?"

"The difference between what's imaginary and what's real."

"Just the same, I promise you'll see me mounted on my ostrich."

"I'd be less surprised to hear him talk to you than to see him obey you," Gordon said with a grin.

Service was not discouraged by such remarks. He set about making a harness for the nandu, and a hood with

blinkers, for his hero Jack had directed his mount by rais-
ing now the right, and now the left blinker. A rope collar,
which the nandu fiercely resented, and reins completed the
outfit.

When the morning of the twenty-sixth of September
dawned clear, Service decided that the time for his ride
had come.

The nandu, hooded like a falcon, stood quite still. The
boys remembered how, when he was caught in the trap, a
blazer thrown over his head had taken the fight out of
him. Now it was easy to lead him to Sports Terrace.
Garnett and Baxter held the cord. After several attempts
Service managed to get astride his bird.

"Let go," he called, with something between doubt and
triumph.

The nandu that still could not see and only felt very un-
pleasant things going on, remained motionless. Service
clamped his legs close to its sides, so he had as firm a hold
as he would on a horse. Then he raised one blinker.

Instantly the creature bounded off toward the woods.
When Service tried to lower the blinker, it shook off the
entire hood as if it were dandelion fluff, and shot on with
the speed of an arrow. For a few moments Service clung
to its neck, then he was thrown. His mount disappeared
in Trap Woods.

"Stupid beast!" Service grumbled, picking himself up.
He had fallen into a patch of thick, soft grass and was
unhurt but furious.

"Wait till I catch you," he shouted. "You just wait . . ."

"You won't ever catch that one again," Doniphan said
laughing.

"Your friend Jack was evidently a better rider than
you," Webb teased him.

"It's just that he wasn't tame enough yet," Service protested seriously. "And anyway, a nandu is not quite the same as an ostrich. It probably has a different character."

"Certainly seems to," Gordon said and added: "Don't feel too badly about it, Service, and next time you read anything you want to imitate in that book by Wyss, take it with a grain of salt."

The day of the nandu-ride brought a turn in the weather, and the boys started planning a trip they had had to put off because of the season. It was to be along the west shore of the lake to its north end. There was no sense heading west to the sea where they had seen no other trace of land. The great question was whether it would be the same in all directions, or whether Chairman Island was part of an archipelago. François Baudoin's map did not indicate this, but then he had not had binoculars. East of French Den the island measured about a dozen miles in diameter. It was really east they wanted to explore, particularly Briant, who had secretly made up his mind to go on this trip with only Moko for company and help. For the moment, the most important matter was to become thoroughly familiar with what lay between Auckland Hill, Home Lake, and Trap Woods, to discover what plant and animal life there was, and how it could serve their needs. Though the weather had definitely changed for the better, it was still too soon to start.

By mid-October they were able to leave off their heavy woolens which Gordon carefully listed, labeled, and put away—for a second winter? The boys kept this thought to themselves and watched him without comment. They still believed, or wanted to believe that, during the summer, some ship would see their flag and that someone would come to find them.

Early in November it grew steadily milder. Doniphan went hunting again and Wilcox, remembering Gordon's warning to save on bullets, set traps. He had to examine them every day and sometimes twice a day, for all too often half-starved jackals got ahead of him and devoured whatever had been caught.

Finally, on the fifth, they decided to set out. This time Briant stayed behind with the Elbees, with Garnett to keep him company. Gordon went with the rest, and Phann, who had played such an important part in their discoveries up to this point, followed him, of course.

The boys took with them rifles, hatchets, and hunting knives. Each had a pistol in his belt. With a view toward saving ammunition, Baxter also carried the lasso and the bolas which he had learned to use very skilfully.

At Gordon's suggestion they had taken the rubber boat. It folded up like a valise and weighed no more than about ten pounds. The map showed two streams or rivers. If these could not be crossed easily on foot, the boat could be inflated; it would take two or three at a time to the opposite bank.

Following the map, a copy of which Gordon had with him, they walked along the west shore of Home Lake. They estimated that, counting the inlets, this must be close to eighteen miles long. Even without any serious delays the trip would take at least three days.

The first two miles were along sandy shore. Phann kept doubling back every few yards to make sure they were coming after him. A stretch of tufted grass, so tall it came to the waist, slowed them up. It proved to be all for the good, however. As they felt their way with their feet, they stumbled into holes hidden by the thick growth. Phann seemed particularly interested in these holes and barked excitedly. When they stooped to see what they were, they recognized them as openings to burrows.

Doniphan immediately cocked his rifle. "There's our dinner!" he announced jubilantly.

"If it'll oblige you by coming out," Gordon said. "Hold on, Doniphan, and don't waste any shots."

"We'll get whatever's in there out without using a single bullet," Wilcox promised.

"How are you going to do it?" Webb asked.

"Smoke them out. The way you do badgers or foxes."

Between the long green tufts, there was enough short, dry grass to make a thick bundle. Wilcox lit it and thrust it into one of the openings.

They did not have to wait long. A dozen or so of half-smothered rabbit-like animals tumbled out. The boys killed two with a hatchet, and Phann took care of three.

"They're tuco tucos!" Gordon exclaimed. "Rabbit South American style. And what a roast!"

"I can cook them right now, if you like," Service offered. With Moko away, he was now chef, instead of just assistant cook.

"Better wait till we make our first stop," Gordon said.

In another half hour they had crossed what seemed like a forest of grass and hit the lake shore again, at a point where a creek ran into it.

It was eleven in the morning, and they had made six miles.

A huge umbrella pine gave fine shade for camping. Cross made a fire between two stones. In the meantime Service skinned and cleaned the tuco tucos. While they were roasting, strung on a long green stick, Phann lay, his tongue lolling out, sniffing at the good smell.

After an excellent meal and a short rest they forded the

creek without difficulty, but found it impossible to keep to the lake shore. It was too swampy. So they walked along the edge of a forest of beeches, oaks, birches, and many kinds of evergreens. Wrens, finches, white-crested flycatchers, and redheaded woodpeckers fluttered among the branches. In the distance they saw condors sailing through the sky, and once even a couple of caracaras, hawks that frequent the coast of South America.

Service, still thinking of his favorite book, hoped to find parrots. Now that his ostrich had been a failure, he wanted to make up for it by teaching a parrot to talk, but none obliged him by showing up.

A little before five in the afternoon they came to a second body of water, a river about forty feet wide. It came from the lake, and they guessed it probably turned north round Auckland Hill and emptied into the Pacific beyond Sloughie Bay. Since it called a halt to their march, they named it "Stop River."

Now the rubber boat could be put to use. They found it could carry only two at a time with safety, so they had to go back and forth a number of times. Phann swam and was over in minutes. The bank was firm. They headed north.

Off and on they had been examining the countryside through their binoculars. Now Doniphan took a look.

"I can see the other shore of the lake!" he exclaimed.

"Let's try and get there before night," Gordon said, when they had all taken a turn at the glasses.

Toward the north, flat, empty land in wavy dunes broken only by reeds and low brush, stretched to the horizon. This part of the island with its vast, sandy miles contrasted markedly with the green forests of the interior. Gordon dubbed it "Sandy Desert."

"If the *Sloughie* had been wrecked here," he said, "we'd have been without food or anything."

Soon the opposite bank was distinctly visible. It seemed forsaken. Except for cormorants, petrels, and grebes, which circled the rocky shore, no living creatures were in sight.

They hesitated whether or not to go on to what seemed the uninhabitable part of the island.

"Perhaps we should leave it for another expedition," Gordon said. "It might take too long now."

"Let's at least go to the end of the lake," Doniphan suggested. "It can't be too far away. See how the curve of the shore is more and more rounded and clear."

"Tomorrow, then," Gordon agreed.

So they camped, although the place was not inviting. There were no trees, and no grass or moss, only the sand to lie on. Since they had no wood to make a fire, they ate what provisions they had in their sacks, wrapped themselves in their blankets, and spent a quiet night in Sandy Desert.

15

Fresh Milk and Horsepower

A dune about fifty feet high rose a few yards from the creek. It would make a good lookout. At sunrise Gordon and his companions climbed to the top for a view of the region.

First they trained their binoculars on the north. If the

sandy desert reached all the way to the Pacific, and that was what the map indicated, they could not expect to see the end of it, for the ocean lay about twelve miles north and more than seven miles east. To go farther in a northerly direction would be of no advantage.

"Well," Cross said. "What would be the best thing to do?"

"Start back," Gordon answered.

"Not without breakfast," Service said decidedly.

"If we do have to go back," Doniphan said, "couldn't it be by another route?"

"We could try," Gordon agreed.

"Then why don't we take a short cut? Cross Sandy Desert to Trap Woods which is only three or four miles to the southwest!"

"Because somewhere or other on that route we'll come to Stop River again."

"What if we do! We can cross it again, just as we did before."

"Where we crossed, the river happened to be calm. There's no telling whether at some other point there wouldn't be strong currents, or whirlpools, or even falls."

"There you go again!" Doniphan said. "Always thinking ahead and seeing trouble."

"You can't see far enough ahead when you don't know the countryside," Gordon answered dryly.

They had a quick meal of leftover meat and a few biscuits, then they rolled up their blankets, slung their bags over their shoulders, and were ready to start.

The day was clear and the lake was ruffled by a light wind. They walked at a brisk pace. Doniphan took off a few minutes to shoot two superb crested bustards. They

had black and red backs and white breasts. This put him
into a good mood again.

When they had crossed Stop River and were in the
woods, Gordon told Baxter to keep his eyes open for a
chance to use his lasso or the bolas.

"They certainly aren't going to be of much use among
trees," Doniphan objected. "And they're no good for
birds at all. I just don't hold with those things."

"Nor do I." Cross echoed his admired cousin.

"Wait and see," Gordon cut short the discussion. "And
in the meantime let's have lunch."

It took quite some time to prepare one of the bustards.
The bird measured close to three feet from bill to tail,
and weighed—they estimated—around thirty pounds. The
roast was excellent, and Phann neatly picked the bones
without getting a single one stuck in his throat.

After a brief rest, the boys entered that part of Trap
Woods which was still unexplored ground. According to
the map, Stop River turned northwest, skirted the end of
the range, and emptied into the Pacific beyond the northern promontory of the bay, the one they had named
False Sea Point. Had they followed the river, it would
have taken them too far from French Den. Compass in
hand they headed due west.

The trees here were not so thick as in the south part
of Trap Woods. Here and there were clearings where
masses of gay wild flowers grew in the sun.

Gordon, whose hobby was botany, noticed a tree with
rather small and scanty leaves on thorny branches loaded
with small red fruits about the size of a large pea.

"That's the *trucla*," he cried. "The Indians use it
for . . ."

"If it's to eat, I'm all for it," Service exclaimed and

popped one of the berries into his mouth before Gordon could stop him.

The next moment he made such a wry face that everybody laughed.

"Uh," he said disgustedly, as he spat out the fruit. "I'm all puckered up inside. It's acid and tastes just awful."

"You didn't let me finish," Gordon said. "It's not meant for eating. The Indians ferment it. We could try it to have something on hand if our brandy should give out."

The fruit was hard to pick because of the many thorns, but Webb solved the problem by shaking the tree, and they filled one of the bags which had held their provisions.

Gordon made two more discoveries to do with plants. When they passed some more of those trees that smelled like cinnamon, he said the bark could be ground up and actually used like cinnamon. It would make a welcome seasoning, and Moko would be very pleased with it. More important was the finding of a *pernettia* whose leaves give a drink very like tea.

"Let's take a few handfuls back with us," Gordon suggested. "Then, if they're good, we can collect enough for months to come. It'll eke out our tea supply."

By four o'clock they had reached the north end of Auckland Hill. Though this was not so high as the part near French Den, it was very steep, an almost vertical ascent impossible to climb. They skirted it in the direction of Zealand River and, two miles farther on, came to a waterfall rushing down through a narrow gorge.

"It's part of the creek, I believe," Gordon said. "The one Doniphan and Briant saw on their first expedition to the lake. And they found the stones François Baudoin must have laid across."

"Why not spend the night here?" Doniphan said. "It's

as good a place as any, what with water, and trees for shelter."

While Service set to work on the second bustard, the others ranged in search of whatever new plants or animals they could find.

Gordon and Baxter went off together. As they approached a large clearing, Gordon suddenly gripped Baxter by the arm and, at the same time, put his finger to his lips. A herd of animals was peacefully cropping the juicy grass.

"Goats?" Baxter whispered.

"Something like goats anyway. Let's try to get them."

"Alive?"

"Yes. It's lucky Doniphan's not here. He would have fired and scared off the lot of them."

They crept closer with soundless steps. The herd numbered six adult animals and two kids. The mother, more alert than the rest, raised her head, sniffed, froze to attention, and was obviously about to run into the woods.

At that moment the bolas whistled through the air. At twenty paces Baxter had hurled them so adroitly that her legs were entangled. She struggled vainly. The rest of the herd had, of course, disappeared.

Gordon and Baxter went up to her. The two kids had remained with their mother.

"She's unharmed!" Baxter declared. "By the way, is it a goat?"

"No," Gordon said, after a critical look. "I should say it's a vicuña."

"Do vicuñas give milk?"

"They certainly do."

"Then long live the vicuñas!"

While they were talking they disentangled the animal

which did, indeed, resemble a goat, only that it had longer legs, a small head that bore no horns, and a short fleece as soft as silk. When the creature realized that the boys were trying to help her, she stopped struggling. Back on her feet, she stood quite still and calm, and allowed herself to be led on a leash. The kids followed their mother, but to make sure they wouldn't stray, Baxter picked them up and carried them.

"This may be the beginning of a herd for us," Gordon said happily.

When they brought back their catch, Gordon leading the grown vicuña, Baxter with a kid under each arm, they were hailed by everyone except Doniphan who regretted the lost chance to make a kill. When he realized, however, how useful the vicuñas would be, he had the grace to admit that, sometimes, it was better to take animals alive, and that the bolas were not to be despised.

When they tied the vicuña to a tree, she did not refuse to graze, as they had feared, so that she would probably take to life in captivity.

This was the first night the boys were disturbed by wild animals. Perhaps these were attracted by the presence of the vicuñas. The bark of a jackal did not worry them because they knew what it was, but they were alarmed by distant growls and even roars.

At three in the morning Doniphan was startled by such a violent outburst that he woke Gordon and the rest.

"Phann's hackles are up and he's afraid," he reported.

"He knows it's not just jackals," Gordon said.

"Then what is it?" Wilcox asked.

"Something bigger, a cougar or a jaguar."

"One's as bad as the other."

"Cougars are less dangerous," Gordon said. "But if

they're traveling in a body, they're something to watch out for."

"We're ready for them," Doniphan announced, his pistol cocked.

"Don't shoot unless you can get a good aim," Gordon counseled. "I think the fire will keep them off."

To judge by the sound, whatever beasts there were, they must be quite near. Phann had regained his nerve and had to be held back forcibly. And still nothing could be seen. Beyond the small circle of light cast by the fire, there was utter darkness.

Suddenly the moving shape appeared at the edge of the circle and light was reflected in two glittering eyes. At almost the same instant a shot rang out.

Doniphan had fired. Pistols ready, the others pressed forward, but evidently the one shot had served to put all the intruders to flight.

"They're off," Cross said.

"Have a good trip!" Service cried.

"Don't you think they'll come back?" Wilcox asked.

"It's not likely, but I'm going to stay on watch till dawn," Doniphan said. "Incidentally, I'm positive I hit one."

He was right. When it was light enough to see, they found a pool of blood. It would have been easy enough to track down the wounded animal, especially with Phann to guide them, but Gordon did not want to venture too far afield, or to waste time. So the question as to whether the visitors had been cougars or jaguars, or some other kind of carnivore, remained unsolved for the time being.

At six they set out for French Den. The vicuñas trotted along with them and gave no trouble at all.

It looked as if the last lap of the journey was to be

without further incident. The way was clear, and the boys did not keep together, but went off here and there whenever something caught their attention. When a shot rang out, they knew Doniphan must have been the one to fire. He and Cross and Webb were far ahead, and the rest ran to catch up with them.

"Heck, I missed it!" Doniphan said crossly. "But I'll get it this time."

"Don't shoot! For heaven's sake, don't shoot!" Gordon shouted.

An animal as big as a horse, which had evidently no notion of attacking them, was making for the woods. Baxter at once hurled his lasso and caught it round the neck. It was so strong that, in its attempts to fight free, it would have dragged him into the forest if Gordon, Wilcox, and Service had not hung on and finally managed to fasten the lasso around the trunk of a tree.

"I should have shot it," Doniphan declared. "It's giving a lot of trouble."

"Shot it when it's just what we need!" Gordon exclaimed.

"What do you mean: 'need?'"

"It's a guanaco," Gordon said contentedly. "A draft animal! They use them in South America to pull loads! Now we won't have to harness ourselves to the cart any more."

Once the guanaco was freed from the lasso, it stood quietly with not the slightest wish to defend itself. It even seemed a little timid.

Gordon thought it belonged to the camel family, but wasn't sure. To the others it looked more like a llama. It was reddish-brown with a narrow neck, small head, and long, rather delicate legs. There was no sign of a hump.

To judge by its gentle manners, it would not be difficult to break it to the harness.

Service had so much faith in its harmlessness that he wanted to ride it then and there and make his entry into French Den astride a splendid mount, but Gordon would not let him take the risk of being thrown.

Their entry was spectacular enough as it was. First of all, the six of them were back safe and sound. Then there was the vicuña with her two kids, and lastly the draft animal.

Costar, who had been playing on Sports Terrace, was the first to see the astonishing procession. His shout brought out the rest, and the explorers were given a joyful and admiring reception.

16

Sugar, Oil, and Christmas

All through November's warm spring weather, the boys were busy constructing quarters for the vicuñas and the guanaco. For the time being these were tied to trees and given plenty of rope to graze. This did very well by day, but at night they had to take the animals in for fear of an attack from the carnivores they knew inhabited the island. But sharing a cave with these new members of the colony was, they discovered, far worse than having the nandu around.

They decided to build a large enclosure at the foot of Auckland Hill, on the lake side, and not far from the second entrance to French Den. All hands were needed for what proved to be a big job. When Baxter caught two more vicuñas, a male and a female, and when another guanaco was trapped, they worked with even better will.

Medium-sized trees, cut and stripped of their branches, were sharpened at one end. They made strong stakes. Planks hammered across would make it impossible for either cougar or jaguar to break down, or to leap over this giant fence. Garnett and Service volunteered to take care of the animals. They saw to their daily supply of food and water, swept out the enclosure and, from time to time, brought in fresh moss and leaves for them to lie on.

In the meantime Wilcox, who had taken to heart Gordon's warning to save on ammunition, had taken a number of pheasants and guinea hens alive.

"This will give us eggs," he announced triumphantly. "All the fresh eggs we want!"

"Milk and eggs! Now I'll be able to make the right kind of dessert for Christmas dinner," Moko promised.

With this tempting prospect, the boys cheerfully went to work on a chicken-yard. Iverson and Jenkins were detailed to see to the fowls.

Eggs and milk was a great addition to meals even before Christmas. There was, however, one eating problem that could not be solved. The sugar supply was running very low. To everybody's annoyance and the Elbees' special sorrow, Gordon was continually urging Moko to save on sugar.

"What can I do!" Gordon defended himself. "We can't make sugar, you know. We don't have sugar beets, and sugar cane doesn't grow here, of course."

And then one morning he found the solution. He was passing trees he had passed dozens of times without noticing anything particular about them except that their leaves had turned an unusually bright clear red. Now he saw they were maples—sugar maples!

"Do you mean the maples are made of sugar?" Costar asked hopefully when he heard the news.

"No, you can't take a bite out of them," Service said seriously. "So don't show your teeth."

"It's the sap that's sweet," Briant explained. "You make a cut in the trunk to let it out. Then you boil it till it thickens, and when it cools, it hardens so you can cut it in pieces."

Everyone ran to the woods to look at these wonderful trees. Only Jack showed little interest even in this new kind of sweet. While the others had been away on their trip, Briant had again tried to make him tell what was wrong with him, and had received the usual answer: "Nothing."

"You ought to come out with it, Jack," he had urged. "I'm your own brother. I have the right to know what's bothering you. And you'd feel better if you got it off your chest."

"I did something," Jack had finally said with downcast eyes, "something nobody could forgive."

"You're just making a mountain out of some molehill," Briant had said eagerly, putting his arm round Jack's shoulder.

The boy had drawn away. "I can't tell you now," he said. For a moment he could not go on talking. His voice choked with tears. "Some other time . . . later," he stammered between sobs and rushed off.

Then and there Briant had resolved to find out what his brother was hiding from him. He would take a long walk with him, or they would go on a trip without the rest.

The boys did have a trip planned for the fifteenth of December, but that was not at all suited to Briant's purpose. But he suggested that everybody go, including the Elbees, so that Jack would not be able to keep to himself and brood.

The purpose of this trip was to replenish the oil supply in French Den. The long winter had taken large toll of it. François Baudoin's candles had been used up long ago, and the two or three dozen new ones they had made of grease drippings carefully saved by Moko, were not only not enough for another winter, they also burned badly. In any case, lanterns, oil lanterns, gave much better light. And a good source of oil was in Sloughie Bay: seal oil!

It was the seals the boys were after, and there was no time to lose. No one knew just when they would migrate to other waters. Gordon had waited this long only because there had been no way to haul barrels of oil from Sloughie Bay to French Den. Now there were the guanacos. After weeks of patient training, Service and Garnett had broken them in. They had not tried to ride them yet, but had harnessed them to the cart and taken them short distances without mishap.

Now the cart was loaded with half a dozen empty barrels, a large tub, various tools and utensils, ammunition, and provisions. The plan was to render the oil then and there instead of enduring the stench of the job at French Den where it might hang on for a long time.

They started out early, but the cart had to travel slowly because, on the right bank of Zealand River, the ground was very uneven. The road—if such it could be called—was even rougher when they had to detour around Bog Woods and find a way between trees. Pretty soon Dole's and Costar's short legs grew so tired that Briant begged permission for them to ride in the cart.

Toward eight, when they were still close to the swamp, Webb and Cross, who had been going on ahead, called an alarm. Doniphan ran towards where the call had come from, and the others followed.

There, in the slimy mud, stood an enormous creature which the boys at once recognized. It was a hippopotamus. Before they could get more than a good look at it, it hid in the reedy swamp.

"What was it? What was that big thing?" Dole demanded.

"Hippopotamus. You know, a river-horse."

"It didn't look a bit like a horse to me," Costar said. "I'd call it a river-pig."

By ten they arrived at Sloughie Bay and immediately saw what they had hoped to find: hundreds of seals were sunning in the sand or waddling between the rocks. They seemed to have no fears, and evidently there was no sentinel seal to warn them of danger. Possibly they had never seen a human being.

Before the boys approached them, they one and all looked out to sea. It was an empty waste of water clear to the horizon. They had not really believed they would see a ship, for apparently their island was not on a maritime route. Yet in his heart of hearts everyone had still thought a miracle might happen.

The seals seemed to be drawn into the water. They were plunging and swimming. It would take the midday sun to bring them ashore in greater numbers again.

After a quick lunch, Briant, Doniphan, Cross, Baxter, and Webb planned the attack. Moko was left in charge of the Elbees. He had also to watch over the guanacos. The younger boys had their hands full holding Phann who would only have been in the way during the seal hunt.

Gordon worked out a plan of battle to cut off retreat into sea. Spaced at thirty to forty paces from one another, the boys then formed a semicircle between the beach and the water. At a signal given by Doniphan all rifles were raised, nine shots rang out together, and nine seals fell. The rest scrambled for the ocean, but Doniphan, obeying his hunter's instincts, pursued them, and the rest followed. By the time the herd had disappeared, there were twenty dead.

Then came the disagreeable job of skinning them and cutting the meat in pieces. Gordon took the lead.

"Come on for some nice smelly work," he called encouragingly.

In the meantime Moko had entrusted Jenkins and Iverson with the guanacos and set up a fireplace. Here he placed the tub half-filled with fresh water. Into this they threw five or six pound chunks of seal meat. A few minutes of boiling, and a clear oil rose to the top. This could be easily skimmed off and ladled into barrels. Some of the boys pinched their nostrils shut from time to time to show what they thought of the smell, but even the sensitive "Lord Doniphan" did not balk at the work or even grumble. By the end of the second day, Moko had filled the barrels with gallons and gallons of oil. The expedition had been a great success.

When they broke camp the following morning, they saw thousands of sea birds swooping down to feast on the remains of the seals. Soon the beach would be picked clean. With a last salute to the signal flag on the mast, with a last look at the empty sea, they started on the trip back.

And now Christmas was coming. Gordon announced that the twenty-fifth and twenty-sixth of December would be holidays. On Christmas morning he got up before the rest and wakened them by firing one of the small cannons of the *Sloughie*. The boom echoed from Auckland Hill.

It was a bright, beautiful day, and the boys spent all morning playing games on Sports Terrace. On the *Sloughie*, equipped for a vacation cruise, they had found tennis rackets and balls, a football, golf balls, and bowling pins. Luckily no quarrels sprang up, and Briant put himself out to keep Dole, Costar, Iverson, and Jenkins amused, since they were too small to join in with the older group. Jack, who could have played with them, preferred to look on.

They had decorated the hall with pennants the night before. When they came in to Christmas dinner the table was spread with a white cloth. In the middle was a Christmas tree, planted in a pot and surrounded by flowers. It was trimmed with small English, American, and French flags in honor of all the nationalities present.

Moko had outdone himself! There was roast rabbit, and a bustard stuffed with aromatic herbs. He had opened tins of vegetables and preserves, and he had made a pudding. And what a pudding it was! In the shape of a pyramid and thick with raisins, currants, and candied fruits. The boys all cheered him for his work. Once the cheering had started, there was no end to it. Gordon was cheered as chief, Doniphan as the great hunter, Baxter as chief engineer, and so on, each boy for his special ability or for what he had done for the good of the colony.

When it was all over, something unexpected happened. Little Costar got up, timid but beaming and, in the name of the Elbees, thanked Briant for all his kindness and care of them.

When the whole table joined in "Hurrah for Briant," he felt embarrassed. These hurrahs found no echo in Doniphan's heart. They rang unpleasantly in his ears.

17

Briant and Jack

A week later it was New Year's Day, 1861. It was midsummer, and ten months since the *Sloughie* had been wrecked. On this day the unspoken question of the older boys was whether there was yet another winter on the island ahead. Briant in particular always had the thought of escape uppermost in his mind. But how? The yawl could not travel far on the open sea, and they had neither the knowledge nor the skill to build a ship that would hold its own on the Pacific. So he pinned his hopes on the east. They must find out whether, from the shore east of Home Lake, they could see a continent or islands forming an archipelago. In any case this region, still unexplored, might provide something or other to add to their diet or make them more comfortable in other ways. He took the matter up with Gordon.

"Baudoin's map is pretty accurate," he said. "But we must remember that he didn't have binoculars."

"Still want to get away, don't you, Briant?"

"Yes, and when all's said and done, so do you."

"Perhaps . . . Anyway, you're right in that we ought to go on this expedition."

"All of us?"

"I think six or seven would be enough."

"That's still too many, Gordon. It would mean going on foot."

"And how do you expect to go?"

"Cross the lake in the yawl. Two, or at the most three, of us."

"Who'll handle the boat on such a longish trip?"

"Moko. He's good at it and can rig a sail. What with sailing when there's a wind and rowing when there's not, we could make good time."

"Sounds all right. And who besides Moko?"

"I'd like to go myself, Gordon. You know I didn't go on that trip north of the lake. Now it's my turn."

"All right. And who's to be the third? I won't suggest Doniphan because you two don't seem to get along."

"As far as I'm concerned I'd gladly have him. He's clever and has plenty of nerve. One of these days, when he finds out I don't want to outdo him, or anybody else, for that matter, we'll be the best of friends. For this trip I have someone else in mind, though."

"Who?"

"Jack. You know how he's been acting ever since the wreck. Keeps to himself. He's done something or other he shouldn't and he won't talk. Perhaps if we're alone for a while I can get him to."

"Take him by all means."

"We shouldn't be away more than two or three days, so it won't need much preparation."

That very day Gordon announced the expedition and that only three would take part in it.

"Of course it has to be Briant," Doniphan grumbled. "And this time his brother, too. The whole clan."

"That's not fair, Doniphan," Gordon remonstrated.

Doniphan did not reply. He went off with his three inseparables: Cross, Wilcox, and Webb.

Moko was highly pleased to turn from cook to sailor. He rigged the sail and remembered to take an extra pair of oars. Two rifles, three pistols, ammunition, three blankets, provisions, and oilskins in case it rained—that was all that was necessary for so short a trip. Briant had a copy of Baudoin's map to which he hoped to add, as he made new discoveries.

On the fourth of February they took off at eight o'clock with a good southwester. Half an hour later Gordon and the others, who were watching from Sports Terrace, saw only a black dot which rapidly disappeared from view.

Moko was in the stern, Briant in the middle, Jack in the bow, at the foot of the mast. For an hour or so they could still see Auckland Hill. Then the wind died down. With only an occasional gust they barely moved.

"Pity the wind couldn't last all day," Briant said.

"It would have been worse if it had veered and carried us in the wrong direction," Moko remarked.

"Moko, you're a philosopher."

"I don't know what that means. I just take whatever comes."

"That's just it! That's why I called you a philosopher."

"Big words or little words," Moko declared. "We have to start rowing or we'll never reach the other shore by night."

"You take one oar, Moko, and I'll take the other. Jack can steer."

"If he steers well, we'll be all right."

"You show me how and I'll do my best," Jack promised. He seemed to be in better spirits.

Moko took in the sail, and they started rowing across what looked like a limitless sea. The compass gave the direction.

Around three o'clock Moko sighted land. Soon they could see trees quite clearly. They stood thick on the low bank, and this explained why Briant had not been able to see this bank from False Sea Point. Evidently the only high part of the island was Auckland Hill.

Rowing was hot work, for the sun had only just passed its zenith. The lake was so smooth and clear they could see myriads of fish twelve or fifteen feet below. They slithered in and out of the long, wavy waterweeds.

By five they had reached the river indicated on the map.

"We ought to name it," Moko said.

"Let's call it East River, since it flows to the east of the island."

"All we have to do now," Moko said, "is to go along East River. It will take us straight to where it empties into the sea."

"It'll have to wait till tomorrow," Briant said. "Better have a rest and spend the night here."

"Are we getting off?" Jack asked.

"Yes, we'll camp under those trees."

They jumped ashore, moored the yawl to a stump, and made a fire at the foot of a tall oak.

Early the next morning they set out again. The tide must have come in half an hour before, and the current was so strong that it carried them along at a swift pace. There was no need to row, but Moko used an oar to keep their raft in midstream.

"If East River is only five or six miles long," he said, "this one tide will be enough to take us to the sea."

"I hope we have the same luck going back."

"If you want to make use of the next tide, we'd have to start back almost the minute we arrive."

"That's no good. We have to take time to see what we've come for: whether there's a continent or another island east of Chairman Island."

East River was narrower and shallower than Zealand River and this explained why the current was so swift. The yawl traveled over a mile an hour. Briant's fear that they might come to a cataract, or that there might be whirlpools, was unfounded. They rode smoothly between dense forests very much like Trap Woods, only that there were hardly any trees except oaks and pines.

Though Briant was not nearly so familiar with plants as Gordon, he recognized a pine about sixty feet high, whose branches formed a sort of umbrella at the very top. Many of its cones were on the ground. They were three or four inches long, pointed at the end, and covered with what looked like shimmering scales.

"You can eat the kernels in those cones!" he exclaimed.

"If it's that kind of pine, it's worth stopping for," Moko said.

With a deft flick of the oar he landed the yawl on the left bank, and Briant and Jack jumped ashore. A few minutes later they were back loaded with cones. The nut-like kernels smelled like hazelnuts. Not only did they taste delicious but—so Gordon told them on their return—they were an excellent source for cooking oil.

During the quarter hour they spent in the forest, Briant and Jack had seen many game birds, a vicuña, a guanaco,

and many nando, enough to show that this part of the
island was as rich in animal life as Trap Woods.

Toward eleven they came to an area where the trees
were fewer and far between. There was a new smell in
the air: salt. One last thin line of oaks, and then they saw
a blue streak on the horizon. They had reached the sea.
The tide still carried the yawl, though more slowly now.
Moko landed on the left bank of East River and, with the
help of a grappling hook, pulled the boat far enough
ashore so that it was solidly bedded in sand.

How different this coast was from that of Sloughie Bay!
The mouth of the river formed a natural port which would
always have water, even at low tide. Had the *Sloughie*
been wrecked here, they would have had an easier time
of it.

Before Briant stopped to examine the terrain more
closely, he trained the binoculars on the east. The bay,
the ocean, were deserted. Not a ship was in sight, not an
island. He handed the glasses to Moko who had been to
sea many times and could tell the difference between
distant hills and clouds or mist.

"Nothing," he said.

Briant was not unduly disappointed. He had expected
this.

"There's no way to leave the island from here," he said.
"Let's call the bay Deception Bay."

"There's always some way to leave," Moko said confidently. "In the meantime, how about lunch?"

"We can take our time about it, because we aren't going
back till the next tide."

"That won't be till evening."

"I'd still like to have another look when the light
changes, and I want to get on top of a rock to see."

"We can travel by night all right. We know there aren't any whirlpools or waterfalls. Besides, there'll be a full moon."

"Fine, Moko. That gives us twelve hours here."

From lunch to supper they looked over the place. The entire shore was made up of enormous rocks and boulders with dozens of caves. Toward two they climbed a tall rock that looked so like a huge bear that they immediately called it Bear Rock. It was about a hundred feet above the little port. From there they could see the forest which reached west to Home Lake. To the south were yellow dunes, to the north the line of the bay and the sandy plain beyond. The only fertile part of the island was the center where the lake was and the rivers which flowed from it to the sea.

Again Briant trained his glasses on the east and first saw nothing but sea and sky. And still he was unwilling to climb down and give up. After a time he looked again.

"There's something to the northeast," he said excitedly.

Moko took the binoculars.

"Yes, there *is* something. It's a whitish patch, but I'm sure it's not a cloud. Anyway, there aren't any clouds at all in the sky right now."

Briant looked again. The white patch did not move or change shape.

"The only thing it could be is a mountain," he said. "And yet mountains somehow don't look like that."

A few minutes later, as the light moved west, the patch was no longer visible. Perhaps it had been nothing but a bright reflection cast up by the water. That was what Moko thought, but Briant had his doubts and stubbornly clung to the possibility of having seen land with a mountain on it.

While Moko prepared supper, the two brothers walked along the shore. When the meal was ready, he called, and when they did not come he went in search of them.

All at once he heard something. It was not a sound of fear or pain. Jack was crying. As Moko came closer, he saw that the younger brother had hidden his face on Briant's shoulder.

Moko did not want to spy on them. He tried to withdraw quietly. But it was too late. He heard what they said.

"You did *that?*" Briant went on, unbelievingly.

Jack sobbed the harder.

"All right, Jack. Now I know. But no one else is to know. No one except you and me."

Moko would have given a great deal not to have been a witness to this scene, the meaning of which he had guessed. They had not seen him, but he knew he would never be able to pretend he hadn't overheard them. He came up to the two.

"I heard . . ." he said.

"So now you know what Jack . . ."

"Yes, and we must not be angry with him."

"Would the others?"

"I don't know. Perhaps it's better not to tell them, like you said. You may be sure that I'll keep my mouth shut."

"Thank you, Moko," Briant said, taking the boy's hand in his. "It's hard to keep things to oneself."

Not another word was said on the subject. Jack was serious and sad, but his restless sullenness was gone. He seemed relieved, almost at peace, now that he had shared his secret with Briant.

Toward ten they started for home. The moon shone on East River. The boys were quiet, each busy with his own thoughts. Even when they reached the lake and found they would have to row through the windless night, they hardly spoke.

At about six in the morning a stiff breeze sprang up and brought them quickly to French Den.

18

Briant and Doniphan

Briant did not tell anyone, not even Gordon, what Jack had confessed to him. For the rest, he gave a detailed account of all they had seen, and spoke of the white patch which had puzzled both him and Moko. Since neither mist rising suddenly from the sea, nor light reflected from the water seemed satisfactory explanations, it was decided that Deception Bay must be visited again, next spring perhaps, and by another group.

In the meantime preparations for the winter were speeded up. Gordon noticed that Briant was doing much more than his share of the work and that he assigned Jack tasks that were often too difficult for his age and his strength. This seemed to have to do with something that had passed between the brothers, but Gordon did not want to ask questions about something which evidently concerned just those two.

To add to the food supply was of prime importance. In February Wilcox reported that salmon were coming in from the sea and swarming up Zealand River. By stretching nets from bank to bank, they caught a great number of them. Salting them away for the winter required so much salt that they had to go to Sloughie Bay several times. There Briant and Baxter had made what they called a "salt trap," a deep square pit which filled up with water at high tide; when the sun had evaporated the water, the salt could be collected.

In March Doniphan, Wilcox, and Webb hunted on South Moors. They had been avoiding this region before because it was swampy. Now Baxter solved the problem of crossing it by making three pairs of stilts. Accompanied by Phann, the hunters crossed Zealand River by yawl, put on their stilts, and walked through the bogs dry-shod. The dog, who did not mind getting his paws muddy, leaped from hummock to hummock, but occasionally he missed and struggled on up to his neck in the watery swamp.

As the three boys stalked along, a band of blazing pink appeared in the blue air: a flock of flamingos, flying evenly spaced. They did not know that these birds always have sentinels to warn them of danger. As Doniphan pointed his rifle, careless of being seen, a call as loud as a trumpet blast rang out. Instantly the birds swerved, and he wasted a shot. He was very much disappointed, for flamingos, four feet from beak to tail, are a delicacy with a taste similar to that of partridge. The boys had to be content with duck, teal, and snipe which Phann skillfully retrieved.

What with quantities of salt meat and fish, stacks of wood which the guanacos had hauled to French Den, and barrels of seal oil, winter comfort was assured.

Over and above the daily work there was an air of excitement in the hall which increased towards the end of May. The boys often separated into groups of twos and threes. They whispered. Even the Elbees went into a huddle and stopped talking when anyone came near. It almost looked as if a conspiracy were afoot.

The point of all this suppressed excitement was that it would soon be the tenth of June: Election Day! On that date Gordon's term as chief of office would come to an end. Who would be the next to govern French Den?

Doniphan had no doubt it would be himself. He should have been elected in the first place, so his followers Wilcox, Webb, and Cross assured him. Doniphan knew that he had the respect, if not the warm friendship of a number of the older boys besides his particular friends. The great question mark was the Elbees. In French Den everyone had a vote and Doniphan realized that he had never paid much attention to his juniors or done anything to increase their comfort or gratify an occasional wish. The Elbees were certainly not for him, but they were definitely against Gordon's being re-elected. Gordon had scolded them too often and too much. Dirty clothes and torn shoes were enough to set him off. Even a lost button! And he was so stingy with sugar! Doniphan and, for that matter, everyone else guessed that the Elbees were all for Briant.

It never occurred to Briant himself that he, who was French, could be the chief in a group of English boys. He took small interest in the coming election, and went on with his work, the first to begin, the last to stop, and Jack worked at an almost equal pace. Only when Gordon insisted, did they take part in the games on Sports Terrace.

One of these, a favorite with everyone, was the game of quoits. It demands a strong arm and a sure aim.

On the afternoon of the twenty-fifth of May, two teams had lined up for quoits: Doniphan, Webb, Wilcox, and Cross on one side, Briant, Baxter, Garnett, and Service on the other.

To understand what happened, one must know the rules of the game:

Two hobs are put up fifty feet apart. Every player has two quoits. These are metal discs with a hole in the middle. The metal is thicker toward the middle, at the hole, and tapers off to the outside rim.

A player casts his quoits first at one, and then at the other hob. If the quoit lands on the hob, it counts two points. If both quoits land, that makes four points. If both quoits fall at the foot of a hob, it counts two points; if only one quoit is close, it is one point.

On this particular occasion, perhaps because Doniphan and Briant were playing against each other, feeling ran high. Each team had won a game. Now the third, deciding game: the rubber.

They had been running even; each team already had five points.

"Your turn, Doniphan," Webb said. "It's our last quoit. We've got to win."

"Don't worry!"

Doniphan took the correct stance, one foot in front of the other, toe on line, body slightly bent to the left to ensure a good throw. He frowned with concentration, gritted his teeth, and threw.

For a split second the quoit hung at the uttermost edge of the hob. Then it fell to the ground. This made a total of six points for his team.

Doniphan could not control his disappointment. He stamped his foot.

"It's too provoking," he said angrily.

"But it doesn't mean we've lost," Cross said.

"Your quoit's right under the hob," Wilcox added. "Unless Briant actually lands his, he'll lose, because it's impossible for his quoit to fall in a better position than yours."

Briant took the stance.

"Watch your aim!" Service cried.

Briant said nothing. He did not want to annoy Doniphan. All he wanted was to have his team win.

Carefully he aimed and threw. The quoit landed square on the hob.

"Seven points!" Service shouted. "The game's ours!"

"Not on your life!" Doniphan shouted back. He came towards them.

"What do you mean?" Baxter asked.

"What I mean is that Briant cheated."

"I—cheat!" Briant had grown very pale.

"Your foot was two paces beyond the line."

"That's not so!" Service protested.

"It certainly isn't," Briant said. "But even if it had been, it would have been by mistake. I won't stand for being accused of cheating."

"You'll have to stand for it." Doniphan shrugged.

"No, I won't. Besides, my foot was exactly on the line."

"That's what you say."

"Come and look at the print in the sand. Then, if you don't admit you're mistaken, you're lying."

"Lying!" Doniphan advanced a step, and Webb and Cross came up behind him. Service and Baxter stood back of Briant.

Doniphan took off his jacket, turned his sleeves up to the elbow, and rolled a handkerchief around his wrist. He looked like a boxer.

Briant had himself under control again. He did not want a fight. It would set the whole colony a bad example.

"First you accuse me of cheating, Doniphan," he said,

"and now you challenge me because I defend myself. You're wrong on both counts."

"I suppose it's always wrong to challenge a person who won't dare accept a challenge."

"Dare! If I don't accept your challenge, it's because I do not wish to."

"That's not the real reason. You're afraid, that's all."

"Afraid! You think I'm afraid of you!"

"Yes, you're a coward."

Briant's only reply was to throw off his own jacket, and roll up his sleeves. He took a step toward Doniphan.

Just as the two were to exchange the first blows, Gordon, whom Dole had alerted, ran up to them.

"Stop!" he called. "Briant! Doniphan! Stop at once!"

"He called me a liar," Doniphan said sullenly. He let his arm drop to his side.

"Only after he said I cheated, and that I was a coward," Briant protested. He stood with his arms crossed on his chest.

"Doniphan," Gordon said firmly. "I know Briant, and I'm sure he'd never start a quarrel."

"And I know you, Gordon, and that you always take Briant's part and take sides against me."

"I take his part when he's in the right."

"And I still say that if Briant won't fight he's a coward."

"And I say you're behaving very badly. How can you go on in this way! Have you forgotten that we're all in a difficult and even dangerous situation? We must stick together."

"Say 'thank you' to Gordon, Briant," Doniphan mocked. "And now come and take a beating."

"I'm still your chief and I forbid it," Gordon said as Briant lunged forward furiously. "Briant, you go back to

French Den. And you, Doniphan, work off your temper anywhere you like, and don't show up until you've calmed down and realize I'm only doing my duty."

"Hurrah for Gordon!" the boys shouted.

The crisis was over, but the incident had deepened the rift between the two factions: Doniphan, Cross, Wilcox, and Webb on the one side, Briant, Baxter, Garnett, and Service on the other. As Election Day approached, everyone tried to guess how, in the light of what had happened, the voting would go.

In the meantime winter had come in good earnest. With the first cold wave, the migratory birds left the island, the swallows before all. Briant, always intent on possible rescue, tried out an old idea: he snared some of them and tied to their necks tiny bags which contained a message about the shipwrecked boys. Then he released the birds. As they headed northeast, he whispered: *"Au revoir."*

The first week in May was so cold that a fire had to be kept going day and night. On the twenty-fifth came the first flurry of snow. According to Baxter's journal, this was a few days earlier than the year before. So the winter threatened to be longer!

By the tenth of June the snow was thick on the ground. Voting was scheduled for the afternoon. Each boy wrote the name of his candidate on a slip of paper and folded it. The slips were dropped into a cap.

In his capacity as chief Gordon opened them and read out the names. The end result was as follows:

> Briant: 9
> Doniphan: 3
> Gordon: 1

Both Gordon and Doniphan had refrained from voting. Briant had voted for Gordon.

Doniphan could not hide his disappointment and irritation, nor Briant his surprise. His first impulse was to refuse. Then his glance fell on Jack.

"Thank you. I accept," he said in a steady voice.

From this day on for a year to come he would be chief of Chairman Island.

19

Skating and Bears

The Elbees were overjoyed that Briant was to be their chief. Gordon was glad and congratulated him, but he worried about what Doniphan's attitude to their new leader would be. It was not likely that he would accept authority from a French boy, and one with whom he had almost come to blows. Gordon was sure that Doniphan was much too intelligent not to realize he was unjust, not to be aware of Briant's sterling character and his devotion to the colony. He was too proud to admit it, though, and had gone off immediately after the election, unable to hide how deeply he was put out by the result of the voting.

As for Jack, one could see he was surprised that his brother had accepted.

"Do you really want to . . . ?" he asked in a low voice.

"Yes. It will give me, it will give us, a better chance to make up for what you did."

During the next few days it became quite clear that Doniphan and his friends were keeping apart from the rest. However, they said nothing which could have provoked criticism, acted much as usual, and did their share in making preparations for the winter. Briant, on his part, was careful not to irritate them, or to exert his authority except when it was absolutely necessary. Even then he always directed his orders or suggestions to a group, never to an individual boy.

Now that French Den was well established, preparing for the winter months was, of course, far less difficult than the year before. Still, there was plenty to do: wood to cut and haul, traps and snares to be attended to. The yawl was put in dry dock and covered with tarpaulin to keep the seams from cracking. Nets were set on the left bank of Zealand River to catch what fish the rough sea might drive toward the interior. The care of the domestic animals took more time now, too, for pheasants and ducks had all hatched broods, and there were young vicuñas which Service and Garnett not only tended, but made much of.

While the weather still permitted, Briant organized an excursion to Sloughie Bay for the purpose of hoisting a new signal. The flag hung on the mast in faded tatters which would never in the world attract the attention of a passing ship. And Briant had never stopped thinking of ships! Ships which would see their signal and come to the rescue.

Since nothing made of cloth would hold up in the snow-storms and wild gales of the cold season, he had cast about for something that would, and remembered certain objects he had seen in New Zealand: the so-called *poi* balls the Maoris there make of compressed rushes tied to strings, and use at festivals when they re-enact the discovery of the country by their ancestors. There are short and long poi balls, the long ones eighteen inches in diameter. Plenty of tough, yet pliable reeds grew at the edge of the swamp.

Baxter took to the poi ball idea at once, and wove a "long" one, a sort of huge balloon which bobbed but did not break since the wind could blow through it. This was raised on the seventeenth of June.

Early in July the freeze set in. They heard jackals every night, and once Phann barked so furiously that they suspected some other, more dangerous, beast nearby. Doniphan and Cross lit brands, rushed to the door, and flung them out into the darkness. They could just make out running shapes without being able to tell what they were. A day later, however, they clearly saw a jaguar, but at too great a distance to try a shot.

By August the lake was solid ice. Moko tested it and declared it would hold anything, even the cart with the two guanacos.

"Why couldn't we skate?" Briant said thoughtfully.

"Without skates!" Garnett exclaimed.

"We could slide," Costar said hopefully.

"No, I mean with skates. Perhaps Baxter could think up a way to make some."

"He's got that look on his face right now," Service said. "The look that means he's figuring something out."

"I've already figured it out," Baxter said simply. "I'll carve a sort of wooden sole and fit iron blades into it. I'll show you how, and anyone who wants to can help me."

Making the skates along with doing the daily chores took a week. On the twenty-fifth of August they were ready.

Briant, Gordon, Doniphan, Webb, Cross, Wilcox, Baxter, Jack, and Jenkins set out to find a good, smooth surface. Iverson, Dole, and Costar were left behind with Moko and Phann. They were not good walkers, especially not in deep snow. Garnett and Service, who had never

skated and thought it was too cold to stumble about learning, decided to keep them company.

About three miles up the river the boys found a long
smooth stretch that ran as far as the eye could reach.

"It's perfect for skating!" Baxter declared enthusiastically.

"Wait a minute before you're off," Briant said, as they
put on their skates. "There's something I want to say, and
that is that you must not go too far. Either Gordon or I
will always be here with a horn, and blow it now and then
to give you the direction. And please, don't try to show
off! I'm not afraid of the ice breaking. It's too thick for
that. What I'm afraid of is that one of you might break
an arm or leg. Think what that would mean in a place
like this! When I blow the horn three times, it'll mean it's
time to go home. So then, please, all start back."

The moment he stopped talking, the skaters tried out
their skill. To his relief, Briant immediately saw that they
were all good at the sport. It made him specially happy
to see Jack take part with evident pleasure. He was a
brilliant skater and did eights and arabesques, or turned
like a top with one leg off the ice, so that the others applauded his performance.

Whether it was Jack's success, or just the wish to get
as far away from Briant as possible, Doniphan began skating very fast and Cross kept up with him.

"I see a flock of ducks over there," Doniphan said. He
had, of course, taken his rifle.

"So do I. It's too far, though. Briant said . . ."

"Don't mention Briant to me. I don't care what he says.
Come on and be quick about it."

They set off at full speed.

"Where are they going?" Briant asked.

"I suppose they've spotted some game," Gordon answered.

"I told them not to go so far."

"I don't think you need worry about them."

"You never know. They're just dots on the horizon."

"They'll be all right. They know how to take care of themselves."

"If the weather holds! You know how a mist can come up all of a sudden."

Only a quarter of an hour later came the proof of what he had said. The horizon quite suddenly disappeared. First there was just a thin drift of mist. Then it thickened. The air over the lake was so milky that one could not even see the west shore.

"There, you see," Briant said.

"Blow your horn!"

Briant blew three notes. The loud blasts rang through the cold air and the skaters, a few of whom had already started back at the first sign of mist, appeared one by one. Only Doniphan and Cross were nowhere in sight.

Briant blew again and hoped that one or the other would fire his gun in reply. The silence remained unbroken, and the mist now hung so heavily one could no longer see even the surface of the lake.

"What shall we do?" Gordon asked.

"We have to find them," Briant said. "One of us must go in the direction they took and blow the horn at intervals."

"I'll go," Baxter offered.

"No, let me!" cried three of the others.

"I'll go myself," Briant said.

"Please, Briant," Jack begged. "Let me go."

Briant gave him a long look.

"All right," he said. "Take the horn with you, and listen for shots."

A moment later Jack had vanished into the mist. Twice they heard him blow the horn. That was all.

"He's too far for the notes to carry," Webb said.

Half an hour went by. There was still no sign of any-one.

"We have to do something," Wilcox said. "They can't stay out there all night. They'd freeze."

"We've a cannon in French Den," Baxter reminded them. "Let's go back and fire it. It'll carry much farther than the horn."

"It's a good idea," Gordon said. "We'd better get going right this minute, though. It's three miles."

In spite of having to trudge through the snow, they made it in fifty minutes.

Baxter put in the charge and they fired. Anxiously they waited. There was no answering sound of the horn, no shot. For the next hour they fired at intervals of ten minutes. Mist is a good carrier of sound, and— as the sun sank lower —the mist thickened.

Moko remembered having heard that a wad of grass soaked in grease and laid over the cartridge would increase the boom. It did. Dole and Costar put their hands to their ears. And still there was no reply. Had Jack, Doniphan, and Cross been anywhere within earshot, they must have heard the repeated roar of the cannon.

At last, towards five, they heard shots.

"They're coming!" Service shouted.

A little later they saw two shadowy figures approaching through the mist. Two! Doniphan and Cross. They had not met Jack, they said. He must have lost his way before he could get to them.

Briant was desperately anxious about his brother, yet he did not say a word of reproach to Doniphan whose recklessness was the cause of all the trouble.

"I should never have let Jack go," he said to Gordon. "I should have gone myself. It's going to be about five above tonight . . ."

Daylight was turning to dusk. A wind sprang up. The mist began to thin. Now, at least, there would be only darkness to cope with.

"We'll make a huge bonfire as soon as it gets dark," Garnett said. "I'll go right now and get more wood from Sports Terrace."

"Wait a minute," Gordon told him. He had been looking fixedly northeast. "I think I see something."

Briant ran for the binoculars.

"It's a dot!" he cried joyfully. "And it's moving!" He passed the glasses to Gordon.

"You're right, Briant. The funny thing is, though, that there are two more dots—behind the first. And big ones!"

A few minutes more and Jack, gliding over the ice like an arrow, was in full view.

"There *is* something else there!" Gordon declared.

"Men?" Baxter asked excitedly.

"I'd say they're animals," Doniphan said decidedly.

"They're very close to him," Briant cried.

"They're almost on top of him."

Doniphan wasted no time answering. He rushed toward Jack with his gun. Two shots rang out. The shapes stopped short. They fell.

"Bears!" Jack gasped, as he came up to the rest. "They were bears! And I didn't even see them till the mist thinned. Then all I could do was to skate as hard as I could. I was quicker than they."

The boys clustered round, everyone eager to do something for Jack's comfort.

In the midst of the general to-do, Cross suddenly said: "Bears! That's funny! We never saw a bear or the sign of a bear on all those many hunting trips we were on."

Although Briant was still absorbed in his brother's safe arrival, part of his mind started working on the mystery of the bears. There had not been any bears around. Cross had said so. He knew. Then where had these bears come from? Across some frozen channel between Chairman Island and nearby land! Another island! A continent!

Jack brought his thoughts back to French Den. "Thanks, Briant, for giving me this chance," he whispered.

Briant nodded to him. Then he went up to Doniphan.

"It was wrong of you to go so far," he said. "I had expressly asked everyone not to. You were the cause of a lot of trouble to all of us. But it was splendid of you—the way you went to Jack's rescue. I want to thank you for that." He held out his hand.

"I merely did my duty," Doniphan said coldly. He did not seem to see the proffered hand.

20

The Colony Splits Up

Soon the only things that reminded the boys of their first skate, were two very fine bearskins in the Hall.

Spring came early. In October the sun shone on young, green leaves. A light wind ruffled the lake.

As the weather grew milder and it was possible to stay outdoors longer, Doniphan and his friends kept more and more to themselves.

"I think they're up to something," Briant told Gordon.

"I don't believe they'd undertake anything against you," Gordon answered. "Doniphan wouldn't dare. Besides, with the exception of Cross, Wilcox, and Webb, we're all on your side, and he knows it."

"Perhaps they're planning to leave us."

"If they are, we've no right to prevent them."

"Gordon! Just imagine them away from here, where everything is so comfortable now. Away on their own!"

"Come to think of it, I noticed Wilcox making a copy of Baudoin's map. At the time I didn't think it important."

"If Wilcox did that, it means they're going."

"It does look that way."

"Gordon! Wouldn't it be better for me to resign? Step aside for you or even Doniphan? That would put an end to all this silly rivalry."

"No, Briant. You can't go back on us. We elected you."

A few days after this conversation—it was the evening of the ninth of October—Doniphan announced that he, Cross, Wilcox, and Webb were leaving French Den.

"So you're deserting us!" Gordon exclaimed.

"It's not a matter of deserting you," Doniphan replied. "We've decided that we want to be by ourselves on another part of the island. That's all there's to it."

"But why?"

"Because we want to do as we like—and not take orders from Briant."

"Will you tell me what, if anything, I've done against you, Doniphan?" Briant asked.

"Nothing. It's just that you're the chief. We've already

had an American governing our colony. Now it's a Frenchman. Next, it will be Moko."

"You aren't really being serious about this!" Gordon exclaimed.

"I'm entirely serious. If the others want someone who isn't English for their chief, let them have him. We four don't."

"Very well, Doniphan," Briant said. "If you, Cross, Wilcox, and Webb want to leave us, you're free to do so and to take your share of provisions and equipment."

"That's what we intend, Briant. We leave French Den tomorrow."

"I just hope you won't regret it," Gordon could not resist saying.

Ever since Briant had returned from his expedition to the east of the island and reported on the numerous caves there, and on how much game there was, Doniphan had been planning to see for himself as soon as the season permitted. It wasn't too far away from French Den to reach it fairly quickly in an emergency.

Doniphan did not count on crossing the lake as Briant had done. For one thing he did not want to ask Briant for the yawl, for fear of being refused. And even if he were loaned the yawl, neither he nor his three friends knew how to manage it. Besides, he wanted to reconnoiter on foot and get an idea of the lie of the land between French Den and the eastern shore. All he asked for was the inflatable rubber boat for river crossings. For the rest, they took two rifles, four pistols, two hatchets, provisions, and blankets. If they found the area round Deception Bay suitable to set up a permanent camp, they would return for the heavier equipment.

After telling Gordon and the others that they would

always be welcome visitors, they said good-bye. When they left at dawn it was in a black mood. At heart they were sorry to go, but were stubbornly determined to carry out their plan.

The gray sky held the threat of rain. The wind was from the northeast. They made only five miles that day and spent an uncomfortable night in the open. In spite of the fire they kept going till dawn, it was very cold.

Since nothing but swamps and dunes lay east, Doniphan decided to follow the lake shore until they reached East River and that part of the route which Briant had already explored. He would make further expeditions later on. In the meantime he dubbed that long, treeless stretch "The Downs."

Towards eleven they stopped for lunch in the shelter of beeches which grew in a little cove. Wilcox had shot an agouti, a creature which looks like an outsize rabbit, and Cross took over the cooking job with a sigh for Moko, or at least Service, to lend a hand.

The forest which bordered the lake was very like Trap Woods, only that there were more leafy trees than evergreens. Doniphan, constantly on the lookout for game, was pleased to see that it was even more abundant than in Trap Woods.

At about six o'clock they called a halt. They had come to a river which must be East River. When they happened on a heap of ashes under a tree they were sure of it. These could only be the remains of a fire which Briant, Jack, and Moko had made. It was easy to build a new fire on the bed of ash. Since Briant had found this a good camping site and spent the night there, they decided to do likewise. Cross, Wilcox, and Webb unrolled the blankets, but they were not cheerful about it. Probably they were thinking of their beds in French Den and, even more, of the games and chatter in the evening. They would even have been glad to hear Garnett play his harmonica off-pitch! But they had made their choice. They had joined up with Doniphan, and Doniphan, who also had his doubts about the wisdom of what he was doing, was too stubborn to give in. Silently they lay and stared into the darkness.

As soon as it was light, Doniphan proposed crossing East River. At this point it was only about thirty feet wide. Since the rubber boat could take only one at a time, it was slow going. Doniphan crossed first, dragging a long line in his wake. When he jumped ashore he threw the end of the line to the other bank where Cross caught it. In this way they traveled over, one by one. Then the boat was folded up. Wilcox carried it on his back like a rucksack. Going down the river in the yawl, helped by the current, would have been much simpler than the tiresome journey on foot. They lost their way several times and were thoroughly tired out by evening. Doniphan stayed awake longest and tended the fire. Finally he, too, fell asleep and did not wake till the sun was well up.

That day they reached the mouth of the river.

Eagerly they scanned the horizon, taking turns with the binoculars. They even climbed the tall rock Briant had named Bear Rock, to get a wider view. They hardly expected to, nor did they see either land or ships. They looked long and carefully for the whitish patch Briant had spoken of, but could not find it. Probably it had been a trick of light, an optical illusion.

"And yet," Doniphan insisted, perhaps to justify his break with French Den, "if Chairman Island is not far from South America, ships which come from the Straits of Magellan and make for ports in Chile or Peru, have to pass east. We've a much better chance of seeing them here than at French Den." Though he said this more out of defiance than anything else, yet he was quite right in believing that ships would be more likely to pass Chairman Island to the east.

Spirits rose when the boys found a number of large, dry caves from which to choose their new home. They shot several ducks, and Wilcox caught a number of extraordinarily large perch only a few yards from the mouth of East River. Oysters and clams abounded. There would be no food problem at any rate.

That night they discussed whether they should return to French Den at once, to fetch the equipment to establish a home in the cave they had selected. It was in Bear Rock.

"There's no point in waiting," Wilcox said.

"But it will be such a terrible job to haul the stuff by land," Webb objected. "Don't forget that Briant crossed the lake in the yawl."

"The yawl would certainly save us a lot of trouble," Cross said. "What do you think about it, Doniphan?"

"You're right, of course. The yawl would save us a lot of time. Moko could sail it for us."

"And what if Moko refused?" Webb said doubtfully.

"Why should he!" Doniphan snapped. "There's no rule about his taking orders only from Briant. Besides, we wouldn't need him for long. It's only a question of getting across the lake."

"He'll just jolly well have to take us," Cross declared. "Besides, I don't believe the cart would be able to get through that thick forest. So the yawl it is."

"And suppose they don't let us have the yawl?" Webb insisted.

"Who wouldn't let us have it?" Doniphan asked angrily.

"Briant. He's chief, after all."

"I'd just like to see him refuse!" Doniphan protested, but he was not so positive as he sounded.

"As a matter of fact," Wilcox said, "I don't think Briant's the sort to put difficulties in our way. So let's start back to French Den."

"Tomorrow?" Webb asked.

"Not just yet," Doniphan said. "I'd like to explore the north part of the island first. It would take only about two days, and it's a region Baudoin didn't know because there's nothing about it on the map. Before we settle here, we really should know what's north."

His friends agreed and, on the fourteenth, they struck out north.

Between the sandy beach and the forest were masses of rock. It was noon by the time they passed the last, and they decided to lunch by a creek which emptied into a bay. Doniphan named it North Creek. It was easy to cross in the rubber boat, and from there they skirted the forest on the left bank. The only new animal they saw was an enormous tapir, a creature one finds near the rivers of South America. Doniphan recognized it at once and did not bother to fire at it. The bullet would have glanced off the thick hide. Besides it was a harmless, rather timid animal, and not good to eat.

They spent the night in a beech wood and continued their journey before dawn. There was good reason for this. The weather seemed to be changing. A west wind blew. Clouds raced across the sky. Toward evening they heard distant thunder. Gradually it grew louder. It came nearer. Lightning zigzagged across the horizon. The wind freshened. They fought their way on.

Toward eight they heard a sound that was not the soughing of branches or the howl of the storm. It was the crash of water on a beach or reef. They had reached the sea.

All of them were exhausted, yet they started running. While there was still a glimmer of light they wanted to see this part of the Pacific and find out whether there was land in sight.

Suddenly Wilcox, who was ahead of the rest, stopped and pointed to something on the beach. When they came up with him they saw what, at that distance, looked like a whale: an enormous blackish mass. As they came closer, however, they saw that it was not a whale. It was a boat! A wrecked boat!

They crowded round it: it was a small craft lying on its starboard side. And nearby in a tangle of seaweed the storm had cast ashore, was something else. Two men were lying there.

They rushed toward them and stopped short. The men lay quite still. As if they were dead. Yes, they must be dead!

Frightened out of their wits the boys ran for all they were worth. They did not even stop to discover whether a flicker of life might still be in those two bodies: whether they could revive them. Helter-skelter the four made for the shelter of the forest.

The moment they arrived there they looked at one another in dismay.

"We shouldn't have left them there," Wilcox said.

"Do you think we ought to go back?" Webb asked in a very small voice.

"We'll have to," Doniphan decided. He had himself in hand again.

"It's so dark now, we'll never find the way either there or back," Cross said.

At his words the storm seemed to grow wilder. Great boughs broke off in the wind, and whole trees were uprooted. The boys made for the beach under Doniphan's direction. Long before they were anywhere near the boat, they had to throw themselves flat on the ground, for the sand pelted them like hailstones.

"We'll have to wait till tomorrow," Doniphan gasped.

Back to the forest they stumbled. It was impossible to light a fire. In any case, it would have been dangerous to do so, for the dead wood lying all about would have caught and started a blaze, a blaze the wind would spread!

Cold and miserable they huddled together. They could not sleep. Besides their discomfort they were beset with questions: What was that boat? Who were those men?

They imagined they heard cries for help, and then again it seemed only the sound of sea and wind.

Doniphan suffered more than the rest. Ever since the wreck of the *Sloughie* he had thought himself wiser, stronger, and more experienced than his companions. Now, at a crucial moment, his courage had failed him. He had run away from people who might not have been beyond help. And there was another thing: the instant he had seen men, grown men, he had realized that he was nothing but a half-grown boy, that he actually knew very little, and was not half so wonderful as he had pretended to himself as well as to his friends.

The night was endless. They tossed restlessly and spoke in whispers, as if someone could overhear them.

"We'll go back and bury them the minute it's day," Doniphan said.

As the darkness thinned, the storm subsided. The clouds

hung low. It might rain before they could return to Bear
Rock. But before they could even think of the return
trip, they must investigate that boat. After they had dug
a grave for the bodies, of course.

They soon saw the capsized craft. But where were the
men? The dead men? They were gone!

The boys searched here and there.

"They couldn't have been dead," Webb said positively.
"They've gone away."

"There aren't any footprints," Cross announced.

"Why should there be!" Doniphan said. "The tide's
washed them away."

"Where can they be?" Wilcox wondered.

"They could have been dead and washed out to sea."
Doniphan sounded impatient. "Let's go and see if anything's in the boat," he added.

It was a launch of the kind merchant ships carry, an
open boat with a deckhouse. The keel was about thirty
feet long. She had been badly damaged by the shock
which had hurled her ashore. All that was left of her gear
was a broken mast and a sail which hung in tatters. There
was not a scrap of food and no tool of any kind in the
forecastle or anywhere else.

They climbed out.

"Hey, look, there's a name!" Webb exclaimed excitedly.

On the stern they read: "*Severn*—San Francisco."

San Francisco! A port in California! The *Severn* had
been an American ship.

As they stood on the coast where the launch had been
wrecked, they saw only limitless sea.

21

Murderers on Chairman Island

French Den was not the place it had been. Doniphan, Cross, Webb, and Wilcox had gone off on their own, and in a hostile spirit. The other boys missed them and were more than just sorry; they worried at what this splitting of forces might mean in some future emergency.

Though Briant was not at fault, he was more upset than the others. He knew those four had left because of him. They had said so quite bluntly.

"They won't stay away long," Gordon tried to comfort him. "Doniphan may be stubborn, but I bet he'll have the sense to come back before the bad season sets in."

Briant nodded, but he was not convinced. Gordon's last words, moreover, had sent his thoughts off on another tack. He was filled with alarm. So his friend was counting on a third winter on Chairman Island! Summer was almost over, and the poi ball rigged on the mast had not brought help, probably because it rose to a height of no more than a hundred feet and so was visible only in a fairly small area.

Off and on Briant had tried to think up some signal which could be hoisted higher. Now it occurred to him that a kite might do.

"We have both canvas and lines," he said. "And if we make it right and big enough, it ought to rise, say, a thousand feet."

"Except when there's not a breath of wind," Baxter objected.

"That's not often. There's almost always a wind."

"We could try, anyway," Baxter agreed.

"One could see it about sixty miles off by day," Briant said. "And if we attach a ship's lantern to the framework, one could see it at night, too."

Everybody was delighted with the idea. To the Elbees a kite was something to play with, and they looked forward to one larger than any they had ever seen.

"Be sure to give it a good, long tail," Costar said.

"And big ears," Dole added.

"We could paint a funny man on it and watch him dance in the air," Iverson suggested.

Baxter and Briant set to work on the kite three days after Doniphan and his three followers had left French Den.

"It's a pity the Swiss Family Robinson never thought of flying a kite," Service said. "Then it would all have been explained in the book."

"It's more fun this way," Baxter replied. "We'll be the first to do it." He sounded quite proud. "Let's give it eight sides, make it octagonal," he added.

The framework was made of the same kind of tough, yet pliant reed they had used to make the poi ball. There were quantities of such reeds on the shore of Home Lake. Once this framework was ready, Briant covered it with a light-weight rubberized material which they had found among the various pieces of equipment of the schooner. This stuff was not merely waterproof: not even air could filter through. For a cord they used a towline which was at least two thousand feet long. The strands of this line were closely knit, so that it was strong enough to withstand considerable traction.

It goes without saying that the kite was provided with

a magnificent tail which was to keep it from tipping to one side or another. The whole thing was so solidly constructed that it could have carried any one of the boys up into space.

Such a large piece of apparatus could not, of course, be managed by hand. They took the second winch from the *Sloughie* and fixed it firmly in the soil of Sports Terrace. Then they attached the line to it.

On the fifteenth all was ready, and Briant decided to fly the "Giant of the Air," as the Elbees called the kite, the following afternoon. To their great disappointment the weather did not permit them to carry out this plan. Both that day and the next were so stormy that the blustering wind would have torn their kite to bits before ever it was up.

Not until the seventeenth, which turned out to be a red-letter day on the calendar of French Den, could they proceed with their experiment.

It was half past one. The kite lay on the ground, its tail spread to its full length. Everyone was waiting for Briant to give the signal to begin.

Just as he was about to do so, his attention was distracted by Phann. The dog suddenly ran to the edge of the forest and began to bark.

"What's the matter with him?" Briant asked.

"Perhaps he's on the track of some animal," Baxter said.

"No," Gordon said decidedly. "That isn't the way he barks when he's scented game."

"Let's go after him and see," Service said.

"We'd better," Briant agreed. "He may have found something important. But we won't go unarmed."

Service and Jack immediately went to French Den and brought back two loaded rifles.

Phann had disappeared in Trap Woods, but they could still hear his barks which became more urgent every moment.

The boys had not gone more than a few yards when they saw the dog. He was standing over something at the foot of a tree. Not an animal! A human being! A woman! Her eyes were closed. Though she had fainted, probably from hunger and hardships, there was something sturdy about her. She was not young. Her dress was of coarse, brown stuff.

"Maybe it's not just a faint," Baxter said in a whisper. "What if she's dead?"

"Watch! You can see her breath come and go," Briant said.

"She's alive all right," Gordon declared. "What she needs is some brandy, and food."

Jack was already racing back to French Den. Within minutes he returned with a bottle and some biscuits.

She stirred. She opened her eyes. The expression of fear in them changed to wonder when she saw the boys clustered about her. When Briant offered her the biscuits she munched them greedily.

Though they could hardly contain their curiosity, they patiently waited for her to revive. Who was she? When she was able to speak, would it be in a language they could understand?

At last she sat up.

"Thank you," she said. "Oh, how I thank you." It was said in English.

Half an hour later Briant and Baxter helped her walk to French Den where they made her as comfortable as they could. As her strength returned, she told them her story.

Her name was Catherine Ready, Kate for short. She was American, from the west of the United States. For the past twenty years she had been housekeeper in the family of William R. Penfield who lived in Albany, the capital of the State of New York.

A month ago, Mr. and Mrs. Penfield had gone to San Francisco to take passage for Chile, where they were going to visit relatives. They left on a freighter, the *Severn*, whose captain was John F. Turner. Kate, whom they regarded as a member of the family, accompanied them.

The *Severn* was a sound vessel, and all would have gone well, had it not been for the newly-recruited crew of eight who turned out to be thorough-going rascals. On the ninth day at sea Walston, their ringleader, aided by Brandt, Rock, Henley, Cook, Forbes, Cope, and Pike, engineered a mutiny and killed the captain and his mate as well as Mr. and Mrs. Penfield.

Forbes, less cruel than the rest, had spared Kate. Evans, the pilot, was allowed to live only because the murderers needed him to navigate for them. On pain of death they forced him to round Cape Horn and make for West Africa. From there they intended to use the *Severn* for trading with other countries.

A few days later—no one knew how it happened— fire broke out aboard ship. There was barely time to stow a few provisions and arms in the launch. Then they left the *Severn* to her fate. Henley was drowned during the escape.

On the night from the fifteenth to the sixteenth, a violent storm arose. The launch was tossed about by towering waves which finally wrecked it on Chairman Island. Forbes and Pike lost consciousness in the sea, and were flung ashore. Kate herself fell a few yards away, with a sandy point in between, so that she lay unseen as well as unconscious.

When she came to, Walston, Brandt, and Rock had already revived Forbes and Pike and set them to guarding Evans. No one had discovered Kate, and she did not move. Once they had left she was going to try to find help.

"Where are we?" she heard Rock say.

"I don't know, and it doesn't matter," Walston replied. "We'll not be here long. When dawn comes we'll go east."

"How about arms?" Forbes asked.

"Everything's here," Walston said. "Five guns and several boxes of cartridges."

"What about Evans?"

"We have to keep him with us. He knows too much. Besides, if we have to repair the launch and go on by sea, he'll come in handy."

"What happened to Kate?"

"Nothing to worry about there. I saw her go down."

"Good riddance."

A few minutes later they left. When she was sure they were well away, she got up cautiously and examined the launch. They had taken whatever there was: five or six pounds of salt meat, arms, tobacco, and several bottles of gin.

Had Doniphan and his friends heard this recital they would have realized why, when they returned to bury the bodies at sunrise, they had found no trace of them.

As for Kate, knowing that Walston and his gang intended to go east, she trudged west until she broke down where the boys had found her.

They listened in breathless silence. Her story was certainly cause for alarm. Up to now, Chairman Island had, in spite of all the difficulties of daily living, been safe. Now, with armed criminals abroad, the picture had changed. What could Briant and the other boys, the oldest of whom was hardly more than fifteen, the youngest still under ten, do against desperate and ruthless men!

Briant, however, had another and more immediate concern. Doniphan and his crowd were in the utmost danger. They knew nothing of the roving crew of the *Severn*. A single shot fired at a bird, would give them away to Walston. They must be alerted at once.

"We must warn Doniphan," Briant said. "Without delay."

"And bring him and the rest back to French Den," Gordon seconded him. "Now more than ever we need to stand together."

"Once they know what's up they'll come," Briant said confidently. "I'll go and get them."

"You, Briant!"

"Yes."

"How will you go?"

"In the yawl with Moko."

"When?"

"Tonight, when we can cross the lake without being seen."

"Let me go, too," Jack begged.

"No. The yawl will have to take us all back, and there's hardly room for six, let alone seven."

"And the kite . . .?" Costar asked wistfully, but he already knew the answer.

"Nothing doing," Gordon said. "If we fly it, the *Severn* gang will see it. As a matter of fact, I think we'd better take down the poi ball."

Kate had listened to this discussion a little impatiently.

She was eager to hear about French Den, and the boys quickly brought her up to date on their adventures.

At eight o'clock Briant and Moko were ready to start. Each took with him a pistol and a cutlass. A breeze helped them cross. Fortunately the night was very dark. Briant kept peering toward the farther shore to see whether there was a camp fire kindled by Doniphan, a fire which would betray him and his companions to Walston.

Toward half past ten he saw a faint flicker.

"Look!" He caught Moko by the arm.

"A camp," Moko whispered. "Doniphan's? Walston's?"

"I have to find out, Moko. Land here."

"Shall I go with you?"

"Better not. Less risk of being seen if I go alone."

They landed. Briant jumped ashore and told Moko to wait. Cutlass in hand, his pistol in his belt, he vanished between the trees.

His steps were all but soundless. Suddenly he stopped. He had seen a low, skulking form. The next instant his ear caught a menacing growl, and then something shadowy and large leaped . . . It was a jaguar.

"Help!" a cry rang out. "Help!" It was Doniphan's voice. Briant raced towards the sound and arrived just in time to prevent Wilcox from firing.

"Stop! Don't shoot!" he called, as he reached Doniphan. Pinned under the jaguar the boy was struggling for his life. Briant hurled himself at the beast which at once abandoned Doniphan and turned on this unexpected attacker.

Briant was only just able to jump to one side. He swung his cutlass so quickly that the animal fell, mortally wounded, but not before it had clawed his shoulder. Blood streamed from the mangled flesh.

"You saved me!" Doniphan said, as he rose shakily.

"You'd have done the same for me," Briant said in a low voice. "Don't let's talk about it. Anyway, there isn't time. We must leave at once." And he told Doniphan briefly what had happened.

"Briant, you're better than I am," Doniphan could not help whispering on the way back. His gratitude had quite swept away his petty pride and his ambition to be first on each and every occasion.

Briant took his hand.

"I won't let go of you till you promise never to leave us again," he said.

"Never! And you can count on me, Briant, from now on, and absolutely."

The yawl, overloaded by the six boys, had to be carefully maneuvered. It was only Moko's skill and experience that brought them safely across.

Just before morning they landed on the bank of Zealand River. The island had become a very dangerous place. But at least they would face the danger together. Reunited they entered French Den.

22

Where Is Walston's Gang?

All the members of French Den colony were together again, plus a new member: Kate, and now everyone got along with everyone else. Whenever Doniphan felt tempted to assert himself, he remembered what his arrogance and obstinacy had led to. It was not easy for him to set the good of all ahead of his own importance, but he was learning. The realization of danger strengthened the bond between all the boys.

There were men on the island, seven armed men. Kate had said that they intended leaving as soon as possible. If they discovered French Den and its supply of tools and provisions, they would certainly not hesitate to take whatever they needed. The boys did not venture beyond Zealand River. Home Lake and Trap Woods were both out of bounds.

"Didn't you see anything on your trip that pointed to Walston and his men?" Briant asked Doniphan.

"Not a thing."

"From what Kate overheard, it's almost sure he went east," Gordon said.

"Yes, but he probably went along the coast while we cut across the beech woods. If you'll look at the map, you'll see that the island makes a wide curve above Deception Bay. That gives Walston and his gang a very large area to roam about without ranging too far from where the launch was wrecked." Doniphan paused a moment. He had thought of something. "Kate," he said urgently, his eyes bright with a new idea. "Try and think back whether at any time you heard anything at all that might tell us just where Chairman Island is situated."

"Briant's already asked me that," she said and sighed. "All I know is that, after the fire broke out on the *Severn,* Mr. Evans took the wheel of the launch and headed in the direction of South America. So Chairman Island can't be too far from there. But I never heard him mention any island at all. Once they did speak of archipelagoes. Since Walston was so anxious to land on the east coast of this

island, I think it must be near some country in South
America, some place he thought he could reach from
here."

"Good!" Doniphan said with great satisfaction.

"If it were a matter of our leaving, then it would be
good," Briant said. "As it is, we can't plan a getaway of
our own before Walston leaves. And I just hope he doesn't
explore round too much before he does. Do you suppose
that, on your trip, you left any traces he might come
across, Doniphan?"

"Traces! Just a heap of ash, perhaps. If he finds it, all
he'll think is that the island is inhabited. He won't know
by whom. More likely than not, he'll be scared and go
into hiding."

"You didn't fire any shots?" Briant persisted.

"No, for once I didn't," Doniphan said and smiled. It
was probably the first time in his life he had smiled at
himself. "And last night when Wilcox was going to fire on
the jaguar, you came along in the nick of time and . . ."

"That's enough about that," Briant said hastily. "Please
nobody hunt for a while, at any rate."

"Since Trap Woods is out of bounds, too, what'll we
do about food?" Cross asked.

"Live on what supplies we have."

"Luckily there's plenty," Moko said.

With the exception of an expedition to take down the
mast with the poi ball, the boys stayed close to French
Den. Though they had not seen even a thread of smoke
to indicate a camp fire, the uncertainty remained. Toward
dusk they would scramble on the rocks beneath which
their cave lay, but even from up there and with binoculars
they saw nothing but darkness.

In the meantime everyone chafed under the new

restrictions which were so necessary, and yet so irritating.
The only regions they had decided were safe were a
stretch of bank along the river, and Bog Woods. Yet
within these narrow limits a new discovery was made,
and this time it was Kate and not Gordon with all his
botany, who pointed out a kind of tree no one had paid
any particular attention to so far. It was fifty or sixty feet
tall. They had found that the wood was loosely knit and
fibrous and burned too quickly to be a good fuel. The
leaves were oblong and ended in a fine point.

"Why, you have cow trees here!" Kate exclaimed,
when she first saw them.

Dole and Costar burst out laughing.

"Do cows eat them?" Costar inquired.

"Of course not. They're called cow trees because they
give milk! Better milk than the vicuñas."

"Can you milk them?" Costar asked, trying to be funny.

"That's exactly what you do," Kate answered quite
seriously.

They went back and told Gordon of the discovery.
He immediately looked up the tree in one of his books
and found that it was a galactodendron. All one had to
do was to make an incision in the bark. He asked Kate
to take him to the trees. The moment he used his knife a
milky sap dripped from the cut into a pail she held ready.
This sap tasted very good. Later they found out it had
other uses than being an excellent substitute for milk.
When they let it coagulate, it turned into a tasty cheese,
and the fatty portion was like beeswax and could be used
to make candles of a much better quality than those they
had made of grease.

When the excitement of finding out the possibilities of
the sap from the cow trees had worn off, the boys grew

restless again. This was the season they should be exploring those parts of the island which were still unknown to them, and here they were, caged up for nobody knew how long.

"We just have to know what's what!" Doniphan said impatiently.

"Let me try and find out," Kate offered. "Let me go east and see if the launch is still there. If it isn't, it means that Walston has been able to repair it, and that they've left."

"What you've suggested, Kate, is exactly what we thought of doing ourselves," Briant said.

"For you it would be dangerous."

"And how about you? Suppose you fell into Walston's hands!"

"I got away once. I'd do it again. Have you thought that it's also possible that I might come across Evans? If I told him about you and brought him here, just think what a help he'd be. Evans can do almost anything."

"If Evans hasn't escaped with all his know-how, it means that he's being held prisoner," Doniphan said decidedly.

"Doniphan's right, Kate," Briant said. "Evans is being watched. He can't get away. However that may be, we'd never let you take such a chance. We'll have to think up something else."

During the next few days this trying to think up something else filled Briant's mind completely. He hardly spoke and was always deep in thought. Several times he and Moko went out on the lake at night to see if they could catch a glimmer of light. If Walston was still on the island he had to make a fire somewhere. They saw nothing, but

then the area they could watch from the lake was very
limited.

If only we could get up really high, Briant thought.
Then we'd be able to locate a fire. It was like running
his head against a stone wall, for he knew there wasn't a
point even high enough to see the other shore of Home
Lake. It would have to be someplace very high . . .

It was then he had his great idea.

"Remember the kite, Gordon?" he said excitedly. "We
didn't get to fly it, and we never did anything about it
afterwards. Now we could use it—to reconnoiter!"

"I don't see how."

"I'll tell you. Years ago I read about an Englishwoman
who went up in a kite specially constructed so it would
hold a passenger. If we enlarge our kite, make it more
solid, and attach a sort of gondola, it will hold one of us.
Then, at night, when it's a couple of hundred feet in the
air, he'd be able to see a fire no matter where on the
island it was."

"It doesn't sound very possible, but maybe it is,"
Gordon said slowly.

When the plan was told the others, nobody laughed.
They looked doubtful and wondered whether Briant could
really be in earnest, but in the end they went along with
his idea. After months on their own, they were so ac-
customed to danger that something that was, perhaps, more
dangerous than anything they had done up to now, did
not seem impossible. And, of course, they realized at once
that it was the only way to see all of the island.

"Will the kite rise with so heavy a weight?" Doniphan
asked.

"We'll make it so it can hold one person."

"How far up do you think it would go?"

"Six or seven hundred feet."

"Let's get on with it!" Service cried. "The sooner the better. I'm tired of being shut up. I want to come and go as I please."

"It's high time I looked after my traps," Wilcox stated.

"And I'm dying to fire a shot for a change," Doniphan said with a gleam in his eye.

"There's nothing to be gained by waiting," Briant said. "We'll start tomorrow."

When he and Gordon happened to be alone for a few minutes, Gordon asked:

"Are you really going through with this?"

"I'm certainly going to try."

"It's a very risky business."

"Perhaps not so risky as you think."

"Only that it's going to endanger somebody's life!"

"That may well be."

"And who do you think is going to take such a risk?"

"You'd be the very first, Gordon—if the lot fell on you!"

"Are you going to decide who's going by lot, then?"

"No. Whoever goes up will have to go of his own free will—for the good of all of us."

"I believe you already have someone in mind, Briant."

"Perhaps . . ."

Briant would say nothing further. Gordon looked at him long and searchingly, opened his lips as if to speak, then changed his mind and gave his friend a little nod of understanding.

23
Up in a Kite

On the morning of the fifth of November, Briant and Baxter set to work. First they needed to know what weight the kite could carry, such as it was. This would enable them to figure out how much bigger they would have to make it to carry a load of a hundred and twenty to a hundred and thirty pounds in addition to its own weight.

Since they intended flying the kite at so low an altitude that it could not be seen from the east shore of the lake, they would be able to make their experiment by daylight. On a pair of scales salvaged from the *Sloughie,* they weighed out sand. After several trials it was found that the mechanism would rise with twenty pounds. Then it was lowered to Sports Terrace.

They proceeded to enlarge and strengthen the frame with ropes raying out from a central knot like the spokes of an umbrella. This enlarged framework required more canvas, and here Kate proved a godsend. The *Sloughie's* stores had included heavy needles and thread for sail repairs. Kate had already taken over the mending for the colony and thereby relieved the boys of a tedious job; now she tackled another kind of sewing and did it very well.

Had Briant and Baxter been better at mathematics, they could have calculated the relation of weight, surface area, center of gravity, the velocity of wind, and the point where the line was to be attached. As it was, they had only their preliminary experiment to go on for a rough estimate. This experiment had, however, demonstrated how strong the line must be under traction, to ensure the safety of the passenger. A line from the schooner proved adequate. It must be remembered that, even in a brisk wind, the "pull" on a kite is moderate provided the point of attachment has been correctly gauged, for on it depends the balance of the kite.

Dole and Costar were very much disappointed when the boys decided not to use the magnificent tail. It was quite unnecessary since the ballast would be enough to keep the kite from taking a header.

After a number of attempts, they found that the best position for this ballast was to attach it to a crossbeam by two ropes, at about one third of the length of the frame, and to let it hang twenty feet below it. As for the main line: allowing for curves, about twelve hundred feet would be enough to allow the kite to rise some eight hundred feet.

To offset the danger of a possible fall caused by a break in the line, they planned to make the ascent above the lake where a good swimmer could easily reach the west shore.

When the octagonal kite was completed it had a surface area of seventy square meters. One of those wicker baskets which serve a variety of purposes on a schooner, proved just right for a gondola to hold the passenger. It was deep enough for a boy of average size to stand in it up to his armpits, large enough to permit him freedom of motion, and its opening was sufficiently wide to allow him to bail out in an emergency.

There was one last problem, and it was not easy to solve: how was the passenger to signal when he wanted to come down?

"We can't use a light," Service said. "Walston might see it."

"How about the horn?" Garnett asked.

"Same objection as to the light," Gordon said. "He'd hear it. Besides, it's doubtful whether sound would carry down so far."

"Why not haul the line in after, say, ten minutes?" Cross suggested.

"It might be at the very moment the passenger's still searching," Doniphan said.

"I've thought of something," Briant said eagerly. "We could bore a hole through a lead bullet, thread it on a cord as long as the line, attach the cord to the gondola, and one of us on the ground hold the end. Then all the passenger need do when he wants to come down, is to let the bullet slide down the cord."

"That would work!" Doniphan exclaimed at once. "It's a clever idea!"

To plan and carry out all the operations involved in this venture took two full days. At the end of the second, conditions were particularly suitable for a tryout. There would be no moon until two in the morning. By nine it was dark. A few clouds drifted across the starless sky. The wind was from the southwest.

Everyone, including the Elbees, stood by to watch and, since this was only a tryout, with no passenger in the gondola, what excitement they felt was fun rather than anything else.

They loaded the gondola with a sandbag which weighed a hundred and thirty pounds. This was more than the weight of any one of the boys. The line was carefully coiled. Doniphan, Baxter, Wilcox, and Webb were posted at a hundred feet from the winch which had already been solidly installed on Sports Terrace. They maneuvered the kite into position. Briant, Gordon, Service, and Cross were to work the winch.

"Ready!" Briant called.

"Here we go," Doniphan replied.

The kite trembled into motion. Little by little it rose close to the wind.

"Line!" Wilcox called.

Slowly they paid out line. Slowly the "Giant of the Air" mounted. It grew smaller and smaller until it looked like a bird far up in the sky. To make the experiment as perfect as possible, Briant and his helpers paid out the line to its full length, so that they could determine the degree of traction. It was normal.

The entire performance had lasted no more than about ten minutes, but bringing the mechanism down by hauling in the line, took the better part of an hour. They landed it without undue jolt. To make sure the wind would not carry it off by night, Baxter and Wilcox offered to take turns standing watch.

All had gone well. They had done what they had set out to do, and now everyone was waiting for Briant to start back to French Den. When he made no move to go and seemed deep in thought, Gordon finally said: "Let's go. It's getting late."

"Wait a minute," Briant said in a far away voice. "Gordon, Doniphan, I've been thinking . . ." He hesitated a moment and then went on quickly. "We've tried out the kite. It's been a great success. The wind's just right. By tomorrow it may have veered. I don't think we should put off the actual ascent till then. We should make it now."

The boys were taken aback. The suggestion was reasonable, and yet the boldest among them stood doubtful and silent.

"Who wants to go up?" Briant asked.

Immediately they came back to life, and the matter in hand.

"I do!" Jack cried.

"No, I . . . I . . ." came a confused chorus.

"Please!" Jack begged in a tense voice. "It has to be me."

"Why you rather than anyone else?" Doniphan demanded.

"Yes, why?" Baxter seconded Doniphan.

"Because I must."

"Must?" Gordon repeated in surprise.

"Yes."

Gordon looked to Briant for an explanation, but it was too dark to see his face. He touched his hand and felt it shaking.

"Will you tell us what all this is about?" Doniphan asked in a firm voice.

"It's because of what I did," Jack insisted. His voice was steady and filled with a determination beyond his years. "Gordon, Doniphan, all of you: it's my fault that we're here, that you're here in this island, away from home. I loosed the lines which secured the *Sloughie* to Auckland pier. I meant it for a joke. Then, when she started drifting and going faster and faster, I lost my head. I didn't call you while there was still time. All of a sudden we were away out at sea . . . The storm came . . ." His voice broke. "So now you see why the least I can do is to risk my life for you. I want to try to make up for . . ."

They had crowded round him. They shook his hand, and put their arms round his shoulders.

"You've already made up in lots of ways!"

"Don't think we'll hold it against you!"

"So that's why you've been heading into danger!"

When the voices had subsided a little, Doniphan said: "If you hadn't done anything else, just going after Cross and me in that fog was enough."

Jack smiled through tears. He looked very calm and very happy.

"Thank you, all of you," he said. "And now I'm off." He walked towards the gondola.

"No, you're not," Briant said loudly and clearly. "That's my job. It's I who am going up. The whole thing was my idea, and I never intended anyone to go but myself."

"I guessed it long ago," Gordon said.

While the boys were still putting up arguments as to who had the most right to go, Briant got into the gondola. When he was comfortably settled, he gave the order to fly the kite.

Riding close to the wind as before, it mounted smoothly. Baxter, Wilcox, and Cross paid out line while Garnett let the signal cord glide through his fingers. In seconds the "Giant" was high up, but this time the onlookers stood tense and silent for, along with the kite, Briant was also vanishing into thin air.

The kite rose steadily. It scarcely swayed from side to side. Briant gripped the ropes by which the gondola was attached to the frame.

What a strange feeling it was to be floating in mid-air! As if an enormous and fantastic bird of prey had lifted him from the earth, or as if he were riding on the back of a huge bat. He was quite calm and so full of immense curiosity that there was no room for fear.

Ten minutes after the kite had left Sports Terrace, a

slight tremor indicated that it had mounted almost as high as the line would permit. When it came to the end of the line there were several somewhat stronger tremors. By this time the kite was about seven hundred feet up.

Briant, who had himself entirely under control, made sure he kept a firm hold on the cord with the bullet. Then he let go of the rope with one hand and adjusted his binoculars.

What he saw below was a dark, confused mass in which it was impossible to distinguish lake, forest, or range. Had he been able to make the ascent by day, he could have seen the whole of the island and beyond, and at last made out if it was part of an archipelago, or whether a continent lay close by. As it was, he could not tell. A few stars were out in the east. For the moment that seemed all. Then he saw something light. It was much too large and much too dazzling for a camp fire. It seemed to move, to flare upwards, but it was, most certainly, very far away. Perhaps not on the island at all. Suddenly Briant remembered the whitish patch he had seen on his first trip to Deception Bay. This fire he saw was in the same direction, and now he knew what it was: a volcano! The white patch had been a glacier, and this was a volcano. Both were at a distance of about thirty miles.

While he was still staring at the flame, his attention was caught by a far smaller, fainter light only five or six miles off. He saw it flicker. Undoubtedly it was a camp fire not far from the mouth of East River. Briant's heart began to pound. His hand shook so that he could hardly hold the glasses. Then he steadied himself and looked again. Yes, Walston and his gang were camped near the little port by Bear Rock. The murderers of the *Severn* were still at large on Chairman Island. Evidently they had not been able to repair the launch. The colony of boys was still in extreme danger. At any time now Walston might explore further and discover them.

Briant had found out all he wanted to know and more. There was no object in staying up any longer. Besides, the wind had freshened. The kite was pitching. To land would grow more difficult with every minute. He let the bullet glide down the cord. In a few seconds it was in Garnett's hand.

As the kite began its descent Briant took one last look toward the east and again saw the bright eruption from the volcano and the camp fire near the shore.

Down below they waited in frantic impatience. Doniphan, Wilcox, Baxter, Service, and Webb all worked the winch vigorously. The wind gained in force, and they felt the sharp tug of the mammoth kite. Three quarters of an hour later they had hauled in the greater part of the twelve hundred foot line. The kite was then hardly more than a hundred feet above the lake.

Suddenly they felt a shock so violent it flung them to the ground. At once they realized what had happened: the line had snapped.

"Briant! Briant!" they shouted, forgetting all caution. There was no answering shout. "Briant!" they called again and listened for a reply in terrified silence. This time he answered. He called, and it was a call for help. His voice grew louder, nearer. Now he was running toward them. He was there.

Jack was the first to throw his arms round his brother who was soaked to the skin.

"Walston's still on the island!" Those were Briant's first words. Then he told them how, when the line broke, he had been close to the surface of the lake. The falling kite had acted as a parachute. Just before it plunged into the water, he had jumped out and swum ashore. Relieved of its ballast it had risen again, and the wind had carried it off like some gigantic piece of wreckage.

24

A Call for Help

Moko, who had been the only one in French Den to remain on guard during the night, prepared a late breakfast, for the boys slept well into the morning. While they ate, they discussed the situation.

"Walston's been on the island fifteen days," Gordon said. "If he hasn't been able to repair the launch in all that time, it can only be because he hasn't the tools. The launch isn't that badly damaged. If the *Sloughie* had been in as good shape after the wreck, we'd have fixed her up in a couple of weeks."

"It's true enough that he hasn't left," Briant said. "But that doesn't mean he has the intention to settle on Chairman Island. Because if he had, he'd have explored the interior long before this, and found French Den." He stopped, looked round in a dazed way, and struck his forehead. "Stupid of me to go on about this Walston business when I have something almost more important to tell you!"

"More important than a gang threatening us?" Cross asked unbelievingly.

"In the long run—yes. Remember that white patch

Moko and I saw from Bear Rock when we were at the mouth of East River?"

"Yes, and Wilcox and I could never get a glimpse of it," Doniphan said.

"Well, it's there just the same, and now I know what it is." And he reported on the fiery glow which must have been the eruption of a volcano. "So there *is* land close to the island," he concluded. "And since the men from the *Severn* very likely know about it, they'll do their best to get there."

The boys listened in silence. Briant's account made a deep impression on them. This wasn't guesswork. It was evidence at long last, evidence that they were not on an island alone in miles of ocean, evidence that other land was near. And right on top of this all-important fact which should have made them happy to bursting, came the black certainty that Walston had not left, that he was actually on his way to them. For, according to where Briant had seen the camp fire, he was near the mouth of East River. In other words, he had advanced some twelve miles beyond the place where the launch of the *Severn* had been wrecked. All he needed to do now to come across French Den was go up the river, arrive at the lake, and skirt it in a southerly direction.

More than ever the boys had to be careful about roving far from their cave. The small area Briant allowed them was the left shore of the river as far as Bog Woods. Baxter and Service camouflaged not only the two entrances to French Den, but also stuck small branches, twigs, and bundles of grass between the stakes and crossbars of the animal enclosures.

The pleasant weather made it particularly hard to stay away from the forest and the lake. From the seventeenth onward, the barometer had been steady on "fair." It grew mild, then warm, and the whole countryside turned green. Soon there were masses of gay flowers and tree blossoms. Doniphan almost panted like Phann when he thought of the hunting, and Wilcox itched to set traps and snares. In the few he did set near French Den, he caught only small birds. One day he found a swallow. It had something round its neck. Anxiously Wilcox took off the tiny bag Briant had attached before the swallows migrated, and opened it. There was nothing on the thin scrap it contained except the words Briant himself had written. The small messenger had not brought an answer. Sadly Wilcox let it go.

With little to do the days seemed endless. Baxter, who was still faithfully keeping the journal in which he noted everything that happened, had almost nothing to report.

On the twenty-first of November, when Doniphan was fishing on the bank of Home Lake, his attention was attracted by loud, harsh sounds. They were uttered by birds, a whole flock of them, as large as crows and evidently capable of making a great noise. They flew in wide arcs that diminished as they dropped lower. After a time they alighted, with more of their hoarse chatter. He did not know exactly what they were, buzzards perhaps, or vultures? But it was clear they had clustered round some dead animal. Since Doniphan himself had not fired a shot in weeks, he became curious, returned to French Den, and asked Moko to take him to the opposite shore of Zealand River in the yawl.

The two went off and, a few minutes later, landed on the grassy bank where they were met with indignant cackles by the birds who had been disturbed in their feast. They flew up, but stayed watching from a nearby tree.

The boys found a young guanaco which could not have been dead more than a few hours. Doniphan examined it. The body was still warm. He found a wound which had not been inflicted by the teeth of a jaguar or, indeed, of any other creature. It was a bullet hole!

"And here's the proof," Moko said. He had probed the wound with his knife and extracted a bullet. It was not of the sort the boys used for hunting. It must have been fired by Walston or one of his men. Doniphan and Moko returned to French Den at once to report their find.

No one was in doubt as to who had shot the guanaco. The question was, when and where. The animal had been discovered near the river. They knew that the guanacos lived and bred on the Downs. This one must have headed for the river in the heat of the chase. Allowing for the time it had taken to run from the Downs to the river, and for the condition they found it in, it was fair to suppose that Walston and his followers were no more than five or six hours from French Den. The situation was, thus, worse than it had been, but not yet acute.

In the south of the island there were dunes and many small streams which cut through long stretches of swamp. It was not a good hunting ground, and had not enough game to supply food for a number of men. Walston would, therefore, be keeping to the Downs. There was one other fact to support this: the sound of shot which had killed the guanaco had not carried to Sports Terrace. The animal must have been hit at some distant point and run a long way before it died. Nor had the boys heard other shots. So the gang was still well away from French Den.

Just the same, the boys took further precautions. They

reinforced the two doors to French Den with crossbars
and lugged in a large number of heavy stones to make an
additional barricade. Outside they built a sort of bulwark
across the narrow patch which led to the cave. In the
shelter of this bulwark Doniphan and those of the boys
who were the best shots, intended lying in ambush as
soon as Walston was signaled.

On the twenty-fourth, they found another and very
unwelcome sign of the nearness of the band. Briant, who
was walking near the river, stepped on something that
crunched under his foot. At first he thought it was a
shell. There were many lying about. But Gordon, who
was right behind him, stopped short and said:

"Wait, Briant. Take a look at this." He stopped and
picked up something.

"That's not a shell," Briant said, after examining it. "It's
the wrong shape, and blackish . . ."

"It's part of a pipe," Gordon said matter-of-factly.

And that's what it was: the black stem of a pipe. Briant
had broken and partly crushed it.

"Whose can it be?" Gordon wondered.

"Maybe Baudoin's?"

"He's been dead for over twenty years. Look, there are
shreds of fresh tobacco, and here . . ." Gordon stopped
again. "Here's the bowl."

They took the pieces of pipe back to French Den, and
Kate immediately identified them as Walston's pipe. So he
had been so close to them a few days, perhaps even only
a few hours, ago. He might be on his way to French Den
that very minute, and when he discovered that the
inhabitants of the cave were boys, the oldest of whom was
barely sixteen, he would not hesitate to take whatever
he needed or wanted.

Following the finding of the pipe the boys took one last measure to safeguard the colony. They rolled the small cannons of the *Sloughie* in front of the two narrow openings which they had cut on either side of the doors to let in light and air. For the rest, rifles and pistols were always kept within easy reach.

"They must be keeping Mr. Evans a prisoner," Kate said sadly. "Unless they've done away with him. But I don't really believe they have because they need him to handle the launch, once they get it going."

On the twenty-seventh of November, after two extremely hot days, the barometer fell. They heard the growl of distant thunder. That evening Garnett and Webb dragged the yawl into French Den. Then they sat up and waited for the storm to break.

Towards half past nine the whole sky rumbled with thunder. Echoes crashed from rock to rock, and Auckland Hill itself seemed to tremble. Again and again lightning split the clouds. It was one of those electric storms without either wind or rain, that may often last an entire night.

Costar and Dole had hidden under their blankets. Iverson and Jenkins were just visible, but started at every roar. Yet there was nothing to fear. French Den was solid and safe—at least from all kinds of weather. From time to time one of the boys got up and opened the door a crack, only to shut it quickly, blinded by lightning. At one point all space seemed afire, and the lake looked like a sheet of flame.

A little before midnight the thunder seemed to lose some of its violence. The intervals between the flashes of lightning grew longer. A wind rose and scattered the heavy clouds. Finally it began to rain, harder and harder.

Torrents of water beat down and pounded the earth and the rocks.

The Elbees went to sleep, and the older boys at last decided to go to bed, too. Phann had been indifferent to the storm. Now, all at once he began to growl, ran to the door, and stemmed his forepaws against it.

"Storm's over," Doniphan said, and tried to calm the dog.

"He's not upset about the weather," Gordon observed. "He hears something . . ."

"And he's never been mistaken yet," Baxter remarked.

"We can't go to bed without knowing what he's excited about," Gordon said.

"All right," Briant agreed. "But nobody's to go out. If there's someone there, we'll defend ourselves from in here."

Everyone took a pistol or a rifle. Doniphan covered the door to the Hall and Moko that of the storeroom. Phann's barking had become almost frantic, and Gordon could not stop him. He tried both coaxing and command, for the dog's noise endangered them all. Now that the thunder had stopped, and there were longer and longer lulls between the gusts of wind, it could certainly be heard outside.

Then came a sharp report which could not be confused with thunder or a bough snapping, or anything else to do with tempest or trees. It was a shot, and it had been fired no more than two hundred paces from French Den.

As they stood armed and ready, and Moko began to roll the stones in front of the door, they heard a cry:

"Help! Help!"

"Don't open!" Briant ordered. "It's a trick."

"Help!" The call came again. This time it was only

steps away. It sounded desperate. Someone was in the utmost danger.

"It's he!" Kate suddenly cried. "Open the door!"

"Who?"

"It's Mr. Evans. I know his voice!"

The moment Moko opened the door, a man staggered in. He was dripping wet and feeling faint. It was Evans, the pilot of the *Severn.*

25

Evans Tells His Story

When Evans appeared so unexpectedly, the boys, one and all, stood as if rooted to the floor.

Now that he was in the cave, the man collected himself almost at once, and went back to the door which, in the excitement of the moment, had been left unattended. It was not even quite closed. He shut it, then put his ear to it and listened. Evidently he heard nothing, for he turned back into the room.

With a common impulse Briant, Doniphan, and Gordon rushed up and clung to him as if to a lifeline. The others crowded as close as they could get. In the light of the lantern he looked them over.

"Boys," he muttered to himself. "Boys and children." Then his eyes fell on Kate, who had kept in the background.

"Kate!" he exclaimed joyfully. "Kate, alive and well!"

He went towards her and took her hand as if to reassure himself on this point.

He was a vigorous, broad-shouldered man of about thirty with a kind and firm face partly hidden by a beard of two weeks' standing.

"God has saved you as he has me," Kate said fervently. "And now you have come just in time to save these boys who have been so good to me."

"Fifteen," Evans said, counting heads. "And only five or six able to put up a real fight, if it comes to it."

"Are they going to attack us, Mr. Evans?" Briant asked.

"Not just yet."

"Tell us how you happened to come here. Tell us about everything," Doniphan begged.

"Not before he's eaten," Kate intervened. "And those wet clothes! We'll have to find something . . ."

"I had to swim across the river," Evans explained.

Briant took him into the storeroom where they found sailors' clothing which fitted more or less. Then Moko served him venison, made several cups of tea, and set brandy on the table.

Half an hour later, when Evans was refreshed, he was not only willing but eager to tell the tale of his escape.

"Only minutes before the launch crashed ashore," he began, "a huge wave washed five of the men and myself into the sea and knocked us against the reefs. Nobody was badly hurt. We all had bruises, and we skinned our legs and arms. That was all. What bothered us more than the sharp reefs was the heavy seaweed. We got tangled up in it. It gripped us like an octopus. I can tell you that, what with the waves still raging and its being so dark we couldn't see what we were doing, we had a devil of a time getting loose.

"Finally we were clear of it and struggled ashore: Walston, Brandt, Rock, Cook, Cope, and I. Two men were missing: Forbes and Pike. We did not know if they had drowned or if they'd managed to land at some other point. As for Kate, I was sure the backwash had dragged her far out, and that we'd never see her again.

"We started looking for the launch, and it took us a long time to find her. She had been wrecked about seven in the evening. It was midnight before we stumbled on her. That was because we first walked along . . ."

"Severn Shore," Briant said. "That's what Doniphan here called it. He and Cross, Wilcox, and Webb discovered the wreck before Kate came our way and told us about it."

"You knew about the wreck before Kate told you?" Evans asked in surprise.

"Yes, Mr. Evans," Doniphan said. "We were there the very evening you were wrecked, and found two men lying on the sand. We thought they were dead, but when we came to bury them the next morning, they were gone."

"That's right," Evans said bitterly. "They surely were gone. If they'd been dead, that would have made two scoundrels less to deal with. Forbes and Pike were cast ashore not far from the launch. Walston and the rest found them and brought them round with a good swig of gin. They had only fainted.

"Luckily for them and unluckily for us they were provided with both food and ammunition. They had been able to save quite a lot when the *Severn* began to burn: salt meat, rifles, pistols, powder, and bullets. As soon as Pike and Forbes were able to walk, Walston decided to head east. Someone mentioned Kate and that, perhaps, one ought to try and find her, but he said no, she'd been drowned and that it was good riddance." Evans turned to Kate. "Where ever were you?"

"Near the launch, but there was a high ridge of sand and so nobody saw me. I kept quiet, and heard what they said. Then, after they were gone, I ran in the opposite direction. I walked and walked. It was day, and then night, and another whole day. I must have traveled nearly thirty-six hours when these boys found me, half dead with hunger, and brought me to French Den."

"French Den?"

"That's what we call our cave," Gordon explained. "After a French sailor who lived here long before we came. We'll tell you all about it later."

"French Den! Severn Shore!" Evans repeated. "I see you've given names to various parts of the island. That was a good idea."

"Yes," Service said eagerly. "The lake's Home Lake, and then there's Zealand River and South Moors . . ."

"You'll have to tell me all the names by and by," Evans interrupted. "Tomorrow perhaps. Now I'd better finish what I have to tell you. There's no saying when . . ." He got up and listened at the door again. "Nothing—yet," he said.

"I'll stay by the door and do the listening," Moko offered.

"Good! Well, to go back to our journey. An hour after we left the launch we reached trees and decided to pitch camp there. For a number of days after that we kept going back to the launch and trying to make her seaworthy again. We had nothing but a hatchet to work with, though. We couldn't put her in shape even for a brief crossing. So we gave it up for the time being and tried to find a region where there was more game and a river or stream. Our supply of fresh water was almost exhausted.

"After walking about twelve miles we found a river . . ."

"That was East River," Cross informed him.

"Good for East River. There, in a bay . . ."

"Deception Bay!"

"So that's what it's called! Well, in Deception Bay there was a natural port between rocks."

"The biggest one's Bear Rock," Costar cried importantly.

"Bear Rock it is, my boy," Evans said with a smile. "This seemed a good place for working on the launch and we decided to haul her there before another storm smashed her to bits. It was hard work, but we made it."

"You mean to say, that the launch is now at Bear Rock!" Briant exclaimed.

"Yes, and I think it's quite possible to repair her. Of course, one has to have the right tools."

"We have them!" Doniphan declared. "All the tools you need."

"That's just what Walston supposed when he found out that the island is inhabited."

"How did he find out?" Gordon wanted to know.

"It was about a week ago. We made a reconnaissance trip along the river—East River," he corrected himself. "After a time we came to its source: an enormous lake and there, on the bank, we found the strangest looking object. It looked like some sort of a frame covered with canvas."

"Our kite!" Doniphan exclaimed.

"It fell into the lake," Briant explained. "The wind must have swept it on. We never saw it again."

"So that's what it was! A kite!" Evans said. "We couldn't make it out, but we were, as you can imagine,

very, very much interested in it. Because that thing hadn't
made itself. It told us that the island was inhabited. That
was all that mattered to Walston. As for me, I decided
then and there to try and make a getaway. There were
people about! If they were savages, I thought, they
couldn't be worse than the murderers from the *Severn*.
Walston seemed to guess what I was planning for, from
that moment on, I was guarded day and night."

"How did they discover French Den?" Gordon demanded.

"I'm coming to that. But first you must tell me what
you were doing with so huge a kite. I'm curious. Was it
to be some sort of signal?"

Gordon quickly told about how they made the kite and
that Briant had gone up in it. Evans looked at the passenger
with an approving glance.

"I call that uncommonly brave," he said. Then he went
on with his story.

"What you must realize is that now Walston had only
one thought in his head, and that was to find out who was
on the island. If the inhabitants were natives, savages, it
might be possible to come to an understanding with them.

"If they were shipwrecked sailors, perhaps they had the
tools we so desperately needed.

"Little by little, with the greatest caution, we explored
the forest on the right lake bank in a southerly direction.
We never saw a single soul, nor did we ever hear a shot."

"That was because, after Kate had told us about Walston,
we did not venture far beyond French Den, and everyone
had strict orders not to shoot."

"You were discovered just the same," Evans told them.
"In the long run, it had to happen. On the night from the
twenty-third to the twenty-fourth one of Walston's men

came within hailing-distance of French Den and, as luck would have it, he saw a light in what looked like solid rock. It must have been your lantern. You had probably opened the door for a moment. He reported his find to Walston at once, and he and several with him, hid in the tall grass which grows near the river."

"We knew," Briant said.

"How?"

"Because I stepped on a pipe, and when I brought the pieces back, Kate said it was Walston's."

"Yes, that's right. He was much put out about losing it. The main thing was that now he knew about you. From his hideout he watched you come and go. Just boys, he said, whom seven men could finish off with not much effort wasted."

"The monsters!" Kate said indignantly. "Didn't it make any difference to them that these were all young people?"

"They wouldn't stop at murdering boys any more than at killing the captain and the passengers of the *Severn*," Evans remarked.

"It's a mercy you got away!"

"It was after Walston spoke of the boys and began plotting an attack on French Den that I had my chance. Walston and the others went to prowl round your cave and left me with only Forbes and Rock. I broke away and made for the woods. They came after me. I was quicker on my feet but, if it came to a showdown, they were armed while I had only my knife.

"The chase went on most of the day. By cutting through the woods I arrived on the left lake shore. From what I had overheard I knew you were on the bank of a river that flowed west.

"I had made over fifteen miles. I was exhausted. They

were gaining on me. Their bullets started whistling round my ears. After all, I knew all about everything. If I escaped I would tell on them. Besides, what would Walston do to them for letting me get away! They had to capture me at all costs.

"It was late in the afternoon, and I hoped they would give up pursuing me when it got dark. But night was still at least an hour off and Forbes and Rock were on my heels. I knew I couldn't last much longer. And then came a stroke of luck: the storm! It made the going harder because the clouds hung low and made a sort of twilight in which it was hard to see. I was beginning to have hope, when I realized that the flashes of lightning showed those scoundrels my whereabouts. I had just reached the river when a shot rang out, and a bullet grazed my shoulder. I made a quick decision: I jumped into the water. A few strokes, and I had reached the opposite shore and crouched in the long grass. Their voices carried to me.

" 'Do you think we hit him?' Forbes asked.

" 'I'd be willing to swear it. He's dead as a dormouse. Walston will say it was good work.'

" 'I'm not so sure. Walston wanted to keep him alive to handle the launch. He wasn't going to kill him till we reached a continent.'

"I'll show you I'm alive, I thought to myself as they went off. I waited a few more minutes. Then, in a lull between two claps of thunder, I heard barking. It gave me the direction to French Den. I called. The door opened . . . So here I am, and now, boys, what we must put our minds to is to rid the island of those murderers."

"Don't you think that maybe we could deal with them?" Gordon asked. "Promise to lend them the tools they need to repair the launch if they let us alone?"

"First of all, they'll laugh at the idea of striking a bargain. They have the force to take whatever they want, and they'll take it, too. Secondly—and this is even more important—when they'd repaired the launch they'd go off in her."

"That's what we want!" Cross said with satisfaction. "Good riddance!"

"Good riddance! And leave us without the launch so that we can't get away ourselves!"

"How do you mean—get away?" Briant asked. "Surely, a launch can't cross the Pacific?"

Evans looked hard at him, then at the rest of the boys.

"Cross the Pacific?" he repeated in astonishment. "Why, where do you think you are?"

"On an island. There's sea all around it," Doniphan said very positively.

"There is to the west," Evans said. "But south, north, and east there are only channels, any one of which can be crossed in sixty hours at the very most."

"The east!" Briant exclaimed triumphantly. "That's where I saw a whitish patch and, when I was up in the kite, a very big and bright fire."

"You saw a glacier and a volcano. We can find them on a map. You are on an island, but it is part of one of the many archipelagoes near the coast of South America." Evans paused and regarded them with a twinkle. "You gave names to the capes, and bays, and rivers of your island," he said. "What did you call the island itself?"

"Chairman Island. We named it for our school," Doniphan replied.

"Chairman Island," Evans repeated after him and chuckled. "Well, that makes two names, for it already had one before you arrived. This is Hanover Island."

26

Well-Laid Plans

At the tip end of the big triangle of South America is the Strait of Magellan named after Ferdinand Magellan, the Portuguese navigator who discovered it in 1520. It is three hundred and fifty miles long, runs between the mainland of South America and the island of Tierra del Fuego, and is the shortest passage from the Atlantic to the Pacific Ocean. Shorter than the strait the Dutchman Lemaire found almost a hundred years later, and free from the pounding storms of the route around Cape Horn.

The Strait of Magellan has everything: mountains, three thousand feet above sea level, forests rich in game, and streams of fresh water. Its coasts are irregular with many bays and inlets which provide natural ports for the ships passing from one ocean to another.

For half a century only the Spaniards used it. After them came the English, the Dutch, and the French. The names of some of the most famous navigators in the world are connected with it: Drake, for instance, and Cook.

This is what Evans told the boys about the Strait as they pored over the map in Stieler's atlas.

"And now look down here at the Magellan Archipelago," he said, pointing to a group of islands. "Tierra del Fuego's the largest. Here are Clarence and Hoste and others named for distinguished mariners. Here, just where the Strait empties into the Pacific, are other groups of islands scattered along the coast. And now," he paused, and then went on with great satisfaction, "look here, beyond the Strait.

See that island separated only by channels from Cambridge Island in the south, and Madre de Dios and Chatam in the north? Well, that's the one you've been on for over twenty months. That's Hanover Island!"

Briant, Doniphan, and Gordon bent over the map and looked curiously at the island they had thought so far away from land and which was actually quite near the coast of South America.

"Why, there's nothing but a channel between us and the mainland!" Gordon exclaimed.

"That's right," Evans said. "But between Hanover Island and South America there are other islands just as deserted, and once you're in South America you'd have to cross hundreds of miles to reach an inhabited place in Chile or Argentina. Besides the hardships of such a journey, there are dangers, too. The Puelche Indians roam the pampas and are not exactly friendly to strangers. It was lucky for you that you did not try to reach the continent, that you did not leave this island where you established yourselves so well. Now, God willing, we'll all leave together."

The boys still couldn't get over it! It seemed hardly possible that the various channels around Hanover Island were no more than fifteen or twenty miles across and that— weather permitting—they could have crossed over in the yawl. The reason why Briant, Gordon, and Doniphan had not seen land on their various expeditions north and east, was that the land lay so low. The only elevated points were the glacier and the volcano. Besides, so Briant observed after studying the map attentively, by mere chance these expeditions had taken them precisely to those parts of the shore which were farthest away from islands. It is true that Doniphan might have seen the southern coast of

Chatam Island from Severn Shore, had the storm not covered it with fog at the time. From the farther end of the Downs, too, the colonists might have caught a glimpse of Owen Island or of the glaciers in the southeast, but they had never gone as far as the farther end. As for François Baudoin's map, which showed that he must have toured the island in all directions, Evans could only explain the fact that he had not indicated land because fog or mist had made for poor visibility. And then Baudoin had not had binoculars!

"If we manage to get hold of the launch and repair her, in what direction would we go?" Gordon asked Evans.

"Not north and not east," Evans replied promptly. "The farther we can go by sea, the better. With a good wind the launch could take us to some port where we'd be likely to have a warm reception. The sea is very rough along that coast, but crossing channels is easy."

"If we did reach a friendly port, would we be able to get back to our own countries from there?" Briant asked.

"I'm sure of it," Evans said. "Look at the map again. If we cross the channels of the archipelago of Queen Adelaide, where do we arrive by Smyth Channel? In the Strait of Magellan! And almost at its entrance is the port of Tamar. Once we're there, we're already headed the way we want."

"And if no ship is ready to take us on, do we wait there?" Briant asked.

"No, we have a better chance farther on," Evans answered. "Do you see that big peninsula Brunswick? It's there, in the Bay of Fortescue, that ships are most likely to put into port. Once we're in the Strait of Magellan, we can land at many points. We don't have to depend on ships bound for Australia or New Zealand."

"So we head for the Strait," Gordon said. "But first we must make the launch seaworthy, and before that we have to settle this Walston business and get him and his men out of the way, so they can't get in ours!"

If only the launch had been where Doniphan first saw it: on Severn Shore! Then they might simply have taken possession of her. Walston who, at the moment, was located fifteen miles from there, would not have seen them. Evans could have taken the launch to the mouth of Zealand River, and up the river to the site of French Den where repairs could have been conveniently made. The launch could then have been loaded with provisions and other necessary equipment, and they could have left the island under Walston's nose, so to speak.

Unfortunately the launch was no longer on Severn Shore. It was at the mouth of East River and could only be taken by force. That was certain. Force would have to be used. The only question was whether to take defensive or offensive action.

"Would you let me look over what you have in the way of arms?" Evans asked.

Under siege the inhabitants of French Den had at their disposition, so he saw, eight guns and the two small cannons. Besides, they had pistols, hatchets, and knives in case it came to hand-to-hand combat. Both storeroom and Hall seemed to him excellently suited for defence. One faced the bank of the river, the other Sports Terrace. The openings which the boys had cut into the walls would permit shooting in both directions.

Evans praised Briant's forethought in having stones ready to roll against the doors.

"Do you really believe they're out to kill?" Gordon said.

"No doubt about it."

"Except maybe Forbes," Kate objected. "He did, after
all, save my life."

"Forbes!" Evans exclaimed. "Whether it was of his own
free will or whether he was influenced by the rest, the fact
remains that he took part in the massacre of the *Severn*.
And when I was trying to escape, he shot at me as if I were
no more than a wild beast. No, Kate. He's no better than
the rest. If he saved you it was because he thought you
might be of some use. Mark my words, he'll be right along
with the rest when they march on French Den."

The boys settled down to waiting. They knew they
might expect an attack any hour now, and yet everything
remained quiet. It was very hard to keep waiting for something which did not come. From the twenty-seventh to
the thirtieth of November there was not the slightest sign
of any disturbance. Evans was puzzled. He knew Walston.
He knew his plans and that he was in a hurry to carry
them out. Then why the delay?

"Perhaps he will try to save ammunition and enter by
ruse," he finally said.

"How?" Gordon wanted to know.

"I've been thinking about that," Evans replied. "And I
believe I've found the answer. Only Kate and I are in a
position to denounce Walston as the leader of a band of
killers and thieves. Now he thinks Kate is dead, and that I
was hit and drowned in the river. You remember how I
heard Forbes and Rock congratulating themselves on doing
away with me. On the other hand, Walston has no reason
to believe that you know anything about him, or even that
there are sailors on the island. If one of them turns up at
French Den you will, so he thinks, regard him as someone
who's shipwrecked and entitled to help. Once this man is

inside French Den, he can let in the rest and save Walston a lot of bother."

"What we should do," Briant said, "is to point a gun at anyone at all who asks our hospitality."

"On the contrary," Gordon said. "We'd do better to tip our hats to him—if we had any."

"Much better," Evans agreed. "Ruse against ruse."

The following day again promised to be without incident. Evans accompanied Doniphan and Baxter about half a mile in the direction of Trap Woods, keeping well behind the trees at the base of Auckland Hill. He saw nothing unusual.

But in the evening, a little before sunset, Cross and Webb who had stood watch on a low rock of the ridge, came running and reported two men. One was coming from the south lake shore, the other from Zealand River.

Evans immediately went into the storeroom and watched for them through one of the openings. Kate stood at the other.

"Rock and Forbes!" Evans said. "And they are going to try to trick you. Just as I thought!"

"What do you want us to do?" Briant asked.

"Receive them politely."

"Receive them! And be polite! To cutthroats!"

"I'll take care of it," Gordon promised.

"Good," Evans said. "Above all, they must not suspect that Kate and I are here. We'll disappear and not show up till the right moment." He and Kate placed themselves each in a niche of the corridor, and the door was closed on them. A few minutes later, Gordon, Briant, Doniphan, and Baxter went walking on the bank of Zealand River. When they ran into the two men, just as they had intended, both parties exhibited the utmost surprise.

Rock and Forbes seemed overcome with exhaustion. From the opposite bank the boys called: "Who are you?"

"We're from the three-master *Severn*. She was burnt, and our launch was wrecked in the south of this island."

"Are you English?"

"No, American."

"And your captain? And the rest of the crew?"

"Dead. All dead. We were the only ones to survive, and we're at the end of our strength. Who are you?"

"Colonists of Chairman Island."

"Then help us. We've lost everything."

"Shipwrecked sailors are always entitled to help," Gordon said courteously. "We'll get you across."

He and Moko took the yawl across and brought the two men back with them.

Walston had certainly not had much to choose from but, so it seemed to the boys, these men were certainly the least confidence-inspiring individuals imaginable. Rock had a narrow forehead, a head flat at the top and protruding at the back, and a big lower jaw. All this made him look remarkably like an ape. Forbes seemed a little more human.

The two played their role perfectly. For fear of questions which they could not have answered without arousing suspicion, they feigned weakness too great to talk, and pleaded only to be allowed to spend the night in French Den.

When they were finally inside, Gordon noted that they could not keep from casting quick, curious glances around to take in their surroundings, and could not hide their surprise at defence equipment so clearly in view. Their eyes dwelt longest on the cannon rolled into position at the opening.

The young colonists would have found it difficult to

continue playacting in the face of Rock's and Forbes' hypocrisy and thinly veiled intentions. Luckily the men also found their role difficult and begged to be allowed to rest as soon as possible.

"A bundle of grass will do for a pallet," Rock said humbly. "We don't want to be in your way. If you have another room . . ."

"Our kitchen's in the storeroom," Gordon told them. "You can sleep there."

When he took Rock and Forbes into the storeroom, the men noted with one shrewd glance, that it opened onto the river. They almost smirked at the way the boys were taken in. What they probably were thinking was that they need not have gone to such trouble to deceive these innocents. Soon they lay in a corner of the storeroom. But not alone! Moko lay close by. This did not annoy them in the least. They exchanged a look which said more eloquently than words that it would be a small matter to strangle him if he were not fast asleep at the time they planned to go into action. They had already agreed on the hour they would open the door to admit Walston and the others, who were waiting near the bank for the happy moment they would make themselves masters of French Den.

It was close to nine, when Rock and Forbes pretended to fall asleep. Moko was stretched out on his pallet, ready to give the alarm. Briant and the rest had remained in the Hall. After they had shut the door from the storeroom to the corridor, Kate and Evans joined them.

"Everything is going to schedule," Evans said. "We must be ready at any moment now."

After two hours had gone by, Moko asked himself whether Rock and Forbes had, perhaps, decided to put off action until the next night. It was then that he heard a slight noise. By lifting his eyelids so little that he still looked asleep, he saw that the men had left their corner. They tiptoed to the door, which had been barricaded with stones, and began taking these down one by one with the utmost care. Had Moko really been asleep he would not have heard them. In a few minutes the door was free. All they had to do to admit Walston was slide back the bar.

As Rock put his hand to the iron, Moko uttered a blood-curdling yell. Rock turned. A hand fell on his shoulder. The lantern light showed him the pilot of the *Severn*.

"Evans!" Rock cried. "Evans—here!"

"Get Forbes, boys!" Evans ordered and, Briant in the van, the four strongest boys pinioned Forbes' arms and threw him to the ground. With a lightning movement Rock drew his knife and rushed at Evans. When he realized that he had barely grazed the pilot's shoulder, he pushed him violently aside, opened the door, and escaped into the night. Evans fired a shot after him. Since there was no outcry, he knew he must have missed.

"The devil!" he muttered angrily. "At least I'll finish off this one." Knife in hand he advanced on Forbes.

"Mercy, mercy!" the wretched fellow groaned while the boys held him down.

"Spare him, Mr. Evans," Kate cried and threw herself between the two. "Spare him because he spared me."

"Very well, Kate," Evans agreed reluctantly. "At least for the moment."

Forbes, now securely tied, was deposited in one of the niches of the corridor.

The barricade in the storeroom was put up again. Every-one watched till dawn.

27

Fight with the Severn Gang

Although they were all tired out from a sleepless night, no one dared take even an hour's rest the next morning. Since ruse had failed him, there was no doubt that Walston, fully informed by Rock, would soon try open action against French Den.

The sun rose and melted the mist from the lake. A light breeze played over the clear water. On both Zealand River and in Trap Woods all was quiet. The guanacos and vicuñas came and went peacefully in their enclosure. The poultry fed untroubled. Phann romped on Sports Terrace and gave no sign of anything untoward.

Evans studied the ground for footprints and found a great number of them. They showed that Walston and his men had advanced in the direction of the river by night and waited for a door to be opened. Evans could not find a trace of blood. Rock had evidently not been wounded.

A question of great importance was where Walston had come from—the south shore of the lake, like Rock and Forbes, or from the north? Where was he likely to be now? Where had Rock joined him?

To clear this up Evans decided to question Forbes, though he did not have much faith in the result. Perhaps Forbes would refuse to talk at all, or he would not tell the truth. There was, however, the slight possibility that the gratitude he must surely feel toward Kate would influence his attitude toward the boys.

"Forbes," Evans said quietly. "I have to know Walston's

plans with which you are undoubtedly familiar. I'm sure you can tell me what he has in mind. Will you?"

Forbes looked down. He did not want to meet the eyes of either Evans or Kate, nor see the boys grouped around them. He was silent.

"Forbes!" Kate pleaded. "I know there is pity in your heart, because you did not kill me. Won't you do something now to save us all? If Walston takes French Den, it will be mass murder."

Forbes did not reply.

"Forbes," Kate tried again, putting all her energy into persuading the man. "Mr. Evans and the boys let you live, though you deserved to die. You've done so much that is bad, but you have some human feeling. Try to do some good. Think of the crime to which you will be party unless you tell Mr. Evans what he wants to know!"

Forbes stifled a sigh. "What can I do?" he asked sullenly.

"I told you. Tell us from what side Walston came."

"From the north of the lake."

"And you and Rock came from the south?" Evans had taken over the questioning.

"Yes."

"Do they know the other part of the island, the west part?"

"Not yet."

"Where do you think they are now?"

"I don't know."

"Is that all you can tell us?"

"Yes."

"And you believe that Walston will return?"

"Yes."

It was clear that Forbes had told all he was going to

tell, though perhaps not all he knew. They took him back into the corridor.

The situation was still as serious as before. Walston might be in Trap Woods. A reconnaissance trip would have to be made. That this would involve danger went without saying.

Evans decided to go with Briant, Gordon, Doniphan, Cross, Wilcox, Service, Webb, and Garnett. The Elbees, and Jack and Kate stayed in the Hall with Baxter and Moko to guard them.

Eight boys against six armed and hardened criminals were at a disadvantage in spite of their superior numbers. Still, each boy had a rifle and a pistol, while Walston had only the five rifles which had been on the *Severn*. Besides, Doniphan, Wilcox, and Cross were excellent shots, far better than the American sailors. Another thing to their advantage was that they had plenty of ammunition, while Walston had only a few cartridges left.

Of one matter they could be certain: there would be no surprise attack from the rear. Forbes had said that Walston was not coming from the south. His answer about the west had been vague, but it stood to reason that Walston had no time for a route which meant making a detour around Sloughie Bay and going up Zealand River. So the attack must come from the north.

It was two in the afternoon when the little troop set out. The doors of French Den were closed but not barricaded so that, in case they were forced to make for shelter, they could enter at once.

Cautiously Evans and the boys skirted the base of Auckland Hill, keeping well behind thickets and groups of trees until they reached the forest proper.

Evans led. He had had some trouble in restraining Doniphan who always wanted to be in the van of any opera-
tion. After they had passed the mound where François
Baudoin lay buried, Evans headed diagonally for the shore
of Home Lake.

Phann pricked his ears and put his nose to the ground.

"He's found a scent," Briant said.

"Lucky I didn't succeed in holding him back," Gordon
said. "Look, he's following a trail."

"And we'll follow him," Evans said. "As quietly as we
can. And you, Doniphan, who are such a good shot, don't
miss! You'll never fire a bullet to better purpose."

A few minutes later they were in Trap Woods.

"Here are the remains of a fire," Gordon said in a low
voice. "There's some charred wood left, and it's still warm.
This must be where they spent the night."

"They were probably here up to a few hours ago,"
Evans concluded. "I think we'd best head for the range . . ."

Whatever else he was going to say was cut off by a
report from the right. A bullet whizzed past Briant's head
and buried itself in the tree against which he was leaning.

At almost the same instant another shot rang out. A
muffled cry, and—no more than fifty paces away—a body
crashed to the ground.

Doniphan had fired. Now he ran after Phann who was
bounding to the spot.

"Come!" Evans shouted. "We can't let him take such
chances alone!" A moment later he corrected himself.
"There's no chance to take. The fellow's dead. It's Pike."

"The rest can't be far away," Wilcox said.

"No. So don't get out into the open. We won't walk
upright. We'll crawl . . . Down!" he ended urgently. "All
the way!"

Three shots came from the left, and Service, who had not thrown himself to the ground fast enough, was grazed by a bullet.

"Just a scratch on the cheek," he said, as Gordon ran up to him in concern. "Get down again."

"We must stay close together," Evans ordered. "There's still Walston and four others. They must be quite near. We'll advance, but in a group. And remember: crawl!"

"Where's Briant?" Garnett suddenly asked.

"Listen to Phann barking," Doniphan cried. "I'm afraid Briant's gone on ahead, and that they've got him." He leapt up from his crawling position and started running in the direction of the dog's barks. In a moment the rest were following. Evans could not keep them back. They rushed from tree to tree and thought of nothing except that Briant needed them.

"Look out!" Cross shouted suddenly and threw himself on his stomach.

Instinctively Evans lowered his head. A bullet passed over him. When he straightened, he saw one of Walston's men running. It was Rock who had escaped from French Den the night before.

"This one's for you, Rock!" Evans shouted and fired. Rock vanished as if the earth had swallowed him up. "What the devil!" Evans cried. "Did I miss him again! Worse luck!"

All this took place in seconds. The dog was now barking close by. Doniphan called: "Briant, Briant, I'm coming!"

As Evans and the rest caught up with Doniphan, they saw Briant coming to grips with Cope. He had forced the boy to the ground and was brandishing his knife when Doniphan, who had no time to fire, hurled himself between. The knife struck him in the chest. He fell without

a sound. Cope fled north. Someone fired after him, but it
was not possible to tell if he was hit. Phann ran on his
tracks a little way, but soon returned.

Briant had picked himself up. He lifted Doniphan's
head, took it between his hands, and tried to revive him.
The boy's eyes remained closed. His face was as pale as
wax. He did not move. Nor did he give any sign that he
felt Evans tear open his shirt which was soaked in blood.
There was a triangular wound on the left side, at about
the fourth rib. The blade had not struck the heart, for
Doniphan was still breathing, but the breath was so faint,
there was reason to fear he had been wounded in the lung.

"We can't take care of him here," Gordon said. "Let's
carry him to French Den."

Evans instantly agreed.

"Right away then," he said. "While we can carry him
with some safety. There seems to be a lull in the fighting."

What with Pike dead, and Cope and Rock out of the
picture, though no one knew how badly they were
wounded, Walston had evidently thought it wiser to retreat into Trap Woods for the time being. What worried
Evans was that he had not actually seen Walston himself,
nor Brandt or Cook, the three most dangerous men of the
band.

Quickly Garnett and Service improvised a litter and
carried the still unconscious Doniphan as gently as possible. The others formed a bodyguard, rifles loaded, pistols
ready. From time to time Doniphan uttered a low groan.

"He mustn't die!" Briant said with intense feeling. "He's
my friend, and he's been wounded because of me."

Slowly the procession approached French Den. When
they were within a dozen yards or so of the door, they
heard shrieks of distress. At a sign from Evans, they set

down the litter, and bounded in the direction of the sounds. What everyone had feared for so long had happened. Walston had attacked French Den.

While Rock, Cope, and Pike had engaged the attention of Evans and his troop, the three others had climbed Auckland Hill and come down by a gorge which took them to the bank of the river, not far from the entrance to the storeroom. Once there, it had been easy to force the unbarricaded door and break into the cave.

What the boys saw was Walston with someone in his arms. He was heading for the river.

"It's Jack! It's Jack!" Kate screamed, running after Walston and clinging to his arm.

Roughly he shook her off.

An instant later Brandt came running in the same direction with little Costar. Baxter threw himself on the man but was repulsed so violently that he rolled on the ground.

Dole, Jenkins, and Iverson were nowhere in sight. Neither was Moko.

Are they all dead? the boys thought. Jack and Costar were being carried off as hostages. Would Walston kill them, too?

He and Brandt were close to the bank. Were they going to swim across the river? No! There was Cook, ready with the yawl. They were going to take Jack and Costar to their camp at Bear Rock.

To shoot would have been to endanger the hostages. Without knowing just what they were going to do when they got there, the boys ran towards the two men to keep them from getting into the yawl. But Phann ran faster. He was ahead. He had reached the river. With one leap he sprang at Brandt's throat. To defend himself against the

dog, the man had to let Costar go. Walston still held on
to Jack.

Suddenly a man dashed out of French Den. Forbes! He
had managed to escape. He was going to join his old companions. That was what Walston thought.

"Here, Forbes!" he called. "You're just in time!"

Forbes ran towards him, but instead of lending a hand
to Brandt, he hurled himself at Walston. Taken completely
by surprise, the man dropped Jack and then, infuriated by
the treachery of one he had counted among his followers,
he buried his knife in Forbes' side.

It all happened so fast that Evans, Briant, Gordon, and
the rest were still a dozen yards off. They saw Walston
try to get his hands on Jack again in order to drag him to
the yawl where Cook and Brandt, who had fought off
Phann, were waiting. Before he could put a finger on the
boy a shot struck him in the chest. Jack had fired! Walston
could only just stagger up to his men who lifted him into
the yawl and pushed off.

They had hardly left the bank when a great boom
thundered over the lake. The volley crackled on the water.
Moko had fired the cannon and put an end to Walston,
Brandt, and Cook.

So now, except for the two who had so mysteriously
disappeared in the tangle of Trap Woods, Chairman
Island was free of the murderers from the *Severn*. At that
very moment, Zealand River was carrying three of them
out to sea.

28

Off in the Launch

When the excitement of the fight had died down, the boys could hardly believe in their success. Looking back, the danger seemed even greater than it had actually been, for after that first engagement in Trap Woods, their chances had vastly improved.

Evans commended each boy for his share in the outcome, and Moko in particular. But Moko could not enjoy the attention given him, for he had realized belatedly that, when he fired the cannon, he might have hit Jack or Costar!

"You didn't though! And you hid Iverson, Jenkins, and Dole," Jack reassured him. "That was clever of you!"

And then Jack was praised for having had the presence of mind to shoot at Walston.

"If I'd had a pistol, I'd have shot him, too!" Costar declared.

Phann was not forgotten either! He was petted almost more than he could bear, and given a very fine marrow-bone to crunch.

All that kept them from being completely happy was Doniphan. He was breathing regularly, a sure sign that the knife had not perforated the lung, but he was very weak. Kate untiringly made him compresses of crushed alder leaves soaked in water, a remedy used in the west of North America, and so prevented the wound from becoming infected.

Forbes was in much worse condition than Doniphan,

for he had been stabbed in the side. His was a fatal wound, and he knew it.

"Thank you, Kate," he whispered when she tended him. "It's no use, though. I'm going to die." There were tears in his eyes.

"Don't give up," Evans told him. "You did a wonderful thing for the boys. Not one of them will ever forget this, or you!"

Forbes looked at the boys. He looked at Kate and at Evans. An expression of satisfaction came into his face and shone in his eyes. During minutes when his pain was not too intense, he spoke to one or the other. Soon he became unconscious. Towards four in the morning he died. They buried him near François Baudoin.

As Doniphan's condition improved they began to think of Rock, Cope, and Pike. They had not much doubt about Pike, but Evans said over and over again, that the other two might well be alive. While they were at large, it would not do to begin work on the launch. Now that Doniphan could be left without anxiety, Evans, Gordon, Briant, Baxter, and Wilcox went off to search for the men from the *Severn*, with Phann to find the scent.

They did not have to search long. Traces of blood led to Cope who was found dead under a tree. Pike's body lay a few yards farther on. That left only the mystery of Rock, whom the earth had seemed to swallow up. Evans, with the dog to guide him, soon got to the bottom of it. After having been hit, Rock had fallen into one of Wilcox's traps, and had died there. Now the long, deep hole, once dug for a trap, was made to serve as a grave. All three were buried in it.

This marked the beginning of a new era for the colonists of Chairman Island. For months all their efforts had been directed toward surviving. Then there had been the *Severn* gang to deal with. Now they could begin to prepare for the voyage home.

The very next day laid their plans. They would have to go to Bear Rock and stay there until the launch was repaired. Evans, Briant, and Baxter would go by way of the lake and East River. On the sixth of December Evans directed the loading of the yawl. They had been lucky enough to find it almost undamaged by the volley from the cannon, and lying in a quiet backwater. With tools, provisions, and arms aboard, they set off in a brisk wind and rapidly crossed the lake. Before half past eleven Briant showed Evans the creek through which the lake flowed into East River. The tide was just right for the yawl to proceed. Not far from the mouth of the river they found the launch, high and dry in the sand by Bear Rock.

After a thorough examination Evans was able to estimate the necessary repairs.

"We have the tools," he said. "But we need timbers and planks to mend the hull. Those, and the other parts of the *Sloughie* we might need, are in French Den. If we could get this launch to Zealand River . . ."

"Do you believe that's possible?" Briant asked.

"If the launch got to Bear Rock from Severn Shore, why shouldn't it go from Bear Rock to Zealand River!"

They agreed to travel along East River. The yawl would drag the launch in tow. They would take advantage of the tide. Evans made the most of the wait by stopping up as many holes as possible with plugs of oakum he had taken with him from French Den. The work went on well into the evening.

They spent a quiet night in the very cave Doniphan had chosen for himself and his friends on their first visit to Deception Bay. At crack of dawn they started on their trip. While the tide was with them, rowing was easy, but at ebb they could scarcely tow the launch. She was weighed down with water which still came in through a number of leaks. Since progress was so slow, and it was five in the afternoon when they reached the right shore of the lake, they decided to camp rather than travel by night. Besides, in this season, the wind tended to die down in the evening and freshen in the morning, so that if they waited till then, they would be able to sail.

And that was that they did. Evans stood ready to cut the line which held the launch in tow if she threatened to submerge and drag the yawl with her, but luckily she remained afloat. Towards three Auckland Hill hove into view. At five they entered Zealand River and soon docked at French Den. They were welcomed with happy surprise for all had thought they would be away for several days at least.

During the short time they had been gone, Doniphan had improved so rapidly that it was hard to keep him from taking part in the repair work. Evans convinced him that it was out of the question. Even just to get the launch on land took a tremendous effort. She was, after all, thirty feet long and six feet amidships, big enough easily to accommodate seventeen passengers.

When she was finally in "dry dock," Evans, a good carpenter, with Baxter as his right-hand man, and plenty of willing helpers, started on the job. And again Kate was indispensable! She tailored the *Sloughie's* topsail to suit the launch, and used spare sails for jib and gig so the vessel would have the proper equilibrium and be able to utilize whatever wind there was.

The work took thirty days. It was extensive and

thorough. Evans wanted the launch in perfect shape so that she could cross not merely the channels of the Magellan Archipelago, but travel hundreds of miles, should it be necessary to skirt the east coast of Brunswick Peninsula as far as Punta Arenas.

This period of repairs was broken only by Christmas which was an even more joyful occasion than usual. Doniphan was almost well, and the prospect of spending the coming winter with people they loved seemed assured.

While work on the launch was, of course, the chief business of the day, other pursuits were resumed. Wilcox, Webb, and Cross went hunting and set traps, so that Moko might have a good reserve of game for the journey. When the question arose as to whether to have any studies, however, the Elbees struck. This was "vacation" they claimed and, with school in the offing, no one had the heart to force them to their books.

Finally, by the end of January, they began to load the launch. This meant making constant choice of what to take and what to leave behind. Briant would have liked to take everything that had been on the *Sloughie*. Evans and Gordon agreed that provisions, arms, and ammunition were the most important cargo. Gordon also remembered to include the money they had found on the schooner. They might have to use it to buy food in case they were forced to land on one of the islands before reaching Punta Arenas or Port Tamar. At the last moment Doniphan begged them to take the two small cannons. Should they prove too heavy, he explained, they could always get rid of them.

"And books!" Briant reminded them. "We'll want the atlas and maps."

"And compass, lanterns, and binoculars," Gordon added.

"Warm clothing," Moko put in. "And if I'm to cook on a long journey, I have to have a stove."

"Ten barrels of fresh water and a couple of bottles of brandy," Evans said in a decided voice.

By the third of February everything was at last in place.

"Do you really feel well enough to sail?" Briant asked Doniphan.

"Perfectly well," Doniphan said. "Besides, you know what they say about sea air. It's supposed to set you up."

The date of departure was fixed for the fifth of February.

The evening before, Gordon released all the animals. The guanacos and vicuñas made straight for the woods, and the various fowls took a few steps out of their chicken-yard, felt the air of liberty, spread their wings and flew off.

"Ungrateful beasts!" Garnett said disgustedly. "After the care we took of them!"

"That's the way of the world," Service said in so philosophical a tone that everyone burst out laughing.

The next morning they boarded the launch and took the yawl in tow. Doniphan kept close to Evans who was at the wheel. Briant and Moko had charge of the sails even though, for the moment, they counted on the current of Zealand River rather than on the wind. The rest, including Phann, posted themselves wherever their fancy led them.

As the launch began to move they saluted French Den, which had sheltered them for so many months, with three loud hurrahs. Gordon was the only one who was sorry to leave what he felt was his island, but he kept this to himself. Soon Auckland Hill was left behind.

They reached the mouth of the river so late that Evans decided to wait for the dawn before setting out to sea.

It would be difficult to pick a way through reefs in the dark.

It was their last night on the island. The wind had died down. When the gulls, and terns, and petrels had settled into sleep among the rocks, the silence was absolute.

Day came. It was so clear that they could see to the extreme point of South Moors. The wind freshened. With swelling sails the launch left the river for the sea.

Eight hours later they were in a channel near Cambridge Island, rounded South Cape, and sailed along the shores of Adelaide Island. Eagerly they scanned the northern horizon, but Chairman Island, their island, was quite out of sight. There was only the sea.

29

Return to Auckland

The weather remained fair. The sea was calm. Even if there had been a storm it would not have raised breakers in these channels that were only six to seven miles wide. They seemed deserted and, as Evans said, that was a good thing, for the natives in this region were not apt to show kindness to strangers. Now and then they saw fires toward the interior of the island, but never near the coast.

On the eleventh of February the launch entered the Strait of Magellan by Smyth Channel. To the right they saw the peak of St. Anne, to the left magnificent glaciers

like the one Briant had seen to the east of Hanover Island
which the boys still called Chairman Island.

All was well aboard. Doniphan had recovered completely and did his share of the many daily chores for, as
Service said, they were still leading the life of Robinsons.

On the twelfth they sighted Tamar. Without stopping
they rounded Cape Tamar and Evans steered southeast
toward the Crooker Peninsula. He was headed to round
Cape Forward and make his way to Punta Arenas via
Brunswick Peninsula. A long way round!

Unexpectedly their journey was shortened.

On the thirteenth, Service, who was standing watch,
shouted: "Smoke to the starboard!"

"Fisherman who've made a fire?" Gordon asked.

"No, that's the smoke of a steamer," Evans replied.
"Land's too far away to see a camp fire."

He had hardly finished speaking when Briant, who had
climbed into the rigging, cried: "A steamer! It's a
steamer!"

The vessel soon hove into view: a steamer of some
eight or nine hundred tons going at a speed of eleven to
twelve knots.

"Now aren't you glad we took the cannon?" Doniphan
said.

They fired it. They were heard. They were seen. Ten
minutes later they were speaking to the captain of the
steamer *Grafton* bound for Australia.

It did not take long to give him the important facts
about the *Sloughie* and her passengers. The loss of the
schooner had been publicized both in England and
America. Everyone knew about it. Tom Long, the
Grafton's captain, was happy to take the fifteen boys on
board together with Evans and Kate. And Phann! He

even offered to take them straight to Auckland, though this meant a detour for him, since he was headed for Melbourne.

How fast the journey was by steamer! They reached Auckland on the twenty-fifth, almost two years after they had been swept eighteen hundred leagues from New Zealand.

It would take pages to tell about their arrival, the joy of reunion with parents who had long ago given up their children as drowned in the Pacific. And now all fifteen boys were back. In minutes the news spread all over town: the *Grafton* had landed the shipwrecked boys! They were alive and well! The entire population turned out to give them a rousing welcome.

Everyone, of course, wanted to know all about what had happened. Doniphan, who had already shown what a good speaker he was when he took part in the discussions in French Den, gave a series of lectures on their adventures, and the journal Baxter had kept so faithfully, sometimes hour by hour, was published in thousands of copies just for New Zealand readers alone. Finally it was reprinted in magazines both in Europe and America, and translated into all languages. Gordon's gift of organization, Briant's devotion to the colony, Doniphan's outstanding courage, the cheerful acceptance of their fate by all the boys, were admired all over the world.

A subscription was taken up, and Evans was presented with a merchant ship which he called *The Chairman*. Moko was invited to be one of the crew, and Evans was declared both proprietor and captain on one condition: that whenever his affairs took him to New Zealand he would make Auckland his home port and visit the families of "his boys."

As for Kate, everyone wanted her to live with them. She had only to choose. She decided to go to Doniphan's home, for she had become very fond of the boy she had nursed and whose life she had probably saved through her care.

The fourteen other Robinsons went back to the ordinary life of schoolboys. And yet they were not quite like their classmates. Facing dangers, having to rely on their own resources, and accepting hard work and discomfort in a cheerful spirit had strengthened their independence and made them self-reliant beyond their years. For that matter, the little boys were almost big by now, and the big boys almost men.